Then his mind drifted to the girl with the curly dark hair who had checked out his books.

She certainly asked a lot of questions. But she had a pretty smile, and he liked the way her mouth moved when she talked. She might be attractive if she didn't wear those thick glasses that magnified her eyes.

One of the old men had called her Callie. Callie Brandt. *Pretty name.*

Lane sighed, thinking of the lonely life he led. It was nice to have someone take an interest in him for a change. Maybe he would spend more time at the library. . . .

But no, he should avoid Callie Brandt and her questions. He planned to stay only three months in Fort Lob gathering information, and then he would move on. Hopefully, no one would find out who he really was.

DONNA REIMEL ROBINSON is a member of JOY Writers, a local critique group. As a pastor's wife, she heads up the music ministry of their church. In her spare time, Donna enjoys sewing, reading, and watching DVDs of *Murder, She Wrote*. The Robinsons have four children, two children-in-law, and three grandchildren. They live in Denver, Colorado. Visit Donna's Web site at www.donnarobinsonbooks.com.

For the Love of Books

Donna Reimel Robinson

Heartsong Presents

This book is dedicated to my wonderful husband, Richard, who always knew I would get published, and to my Savior, Jesus Christ, who called me to write according to His own purpose.

A special thanks to my JOY Writer critique partners: Kathy Kovach, Paula Moldenhauer, Holly Armstrong, Margie Vawter, Bonnie Doran, Lynnette Horner, Heather Tipton, Jill Hups, and Marla Benroth. Also, thanks to Nancy Jo Jenkins for your prayers. And thank you, JoAnne Simmons, Rachel Overton, and April Frazier, for your hard work in making this book a reality.

A note from the Author:
I love to hear from my readers! You may correspond with me by writing:

Donna Reimel Robinson
Author Relations
PO Box 721
Uhrichsville, OH 44683

ISBN 978-1-60260-302-8

FOR THE LOVE OF BOOKS

Our mission is to publish and distribute inspirational products offering exceptional value and biblical encouragement to the masses.

PRINTED IN THE U.S.A.

one

"I loved this book when I was your age." Callie turned over a worn copy of *Go, Dog. Go!* and ran the bar code under the computer's scanner. "It's due back in two weeks, on Friday, August fifteenth." She smiled at six-year-old Tiffany as she handed her the slim volume.

"Thanths, Callie," Tiffany lisped. One of her front teeth was missing.

Callie watched the girl's braids bounce as she skipped out the front door of the Henry Dorsey-Smythe Memorial Library. *That was me twenty years ago.* She sighed. Her love of books had probably ruined her eyes—just as Grandma had warned her—and now she wore thick glasses. But she still read every chance she could get.

Pulling the tail of her green Dorsey-Smythe polo shirt over her jeans, Callie perched on the tall stool behind the checkout counter. The library was housed in an old Victorian mansion, and the wooden front door had a beveled oval window that Callie loved. She often gazed through it at the main street of Fort Lob, Wyoming.

The door closed behind Tiffany and opened a moment later as Agatha Collingsworth stepped inside. Agatha was tall, and her pink-tinted beehive hairdo barely cleared the horizontal beam of the door frame. She wore her usual outfit—stonewashed jeans, which puffed out at her thighs, and an oversize T-shirt. DON'T MESS WITH TEXAS was emblazoned across her ample bosom.

"Howdy, Callie!" Agatha's husky voice resounded against

the high ceiling as she approached the checkout counter. "How ya'll doing, sugar? I'm here to collect my book."

"Okay, Aggie." Callie turned to the shelf of reserved books behind her. "Your order came in yesterday."

"Yeah, Lucille called last night after I got home from The Beauty Spot and told me to pick up that booger as soon as possible. She don't like folks leaving their books."

"Here it is." Callie pulled it off the shelf and glanced at the title—*Fixing Big Hair the Texas Way*. The model on the cover, who had hair bigger than Aggie's, must have posed for that picture in the mid-1960s. "Looks like your kind of book."

"Oh, I was so excited when I noticed this book in an old catalog." Aggie's gold bangle bracelets clinked as she handed Callie her library card. "Folks around here have such flat hair, and I never could get anyone interested in real style. When I saw this little gem, I had Lucille call the Casper library right away. Wouldn't you know it? They had a copy in their old books section."

Callie ran the bar code under the scanner. Not many people could get away with calling the head librarian *Lucille*. A person had to be at least sixty. "I'm glad Miss Penwell found it for you."

"Lucille can find anything." Aggie took her book. "I have to hustle back to The Beauty Spot. I left your sister minding the store all by her lonesome, and we usually have a crowd on Friday afternoons."

Callie tried to keep a straight face. "I bet you'll have two or three customers wanting their hair done for the weekend."

Aggie's dark eyes danced as she let out a throaty chuckle. "Oh, Callie! Sometimes we have eight! And that's almost more than Tonya and I can handle in one afternoon." She strode back outside, her big hair safely clearing the doorway.

Smiling, Callie placed her chin in her hand. She loved working at the library. When she was a little girl, she pretended this mansion was her home. Mildred Dorsey-Smythe, the maiden daughter of Henry, had willed the house to the town of Fort Lob for the specific purpose of providing a library for the residents. The front entrance alcove made a perfect place for the tall wooden counter that served as a checkout desk. It was tucked next to the sweeping staircase that accessed the reference rooms upstairs.

But Mildred had died almost fifty years ago, and now the house was over a hundred. The wooden stairs, scuffed by generations of children, competed with the old chipped banisters, which had been repainted a dozen times.

Grabbing the cart laden with books to be reshelved, Callie wheeled it past the staircase into the main room of the library. She glanced up at the ceiling molding that ran around the perimeter of the room. A chunk had fallen out last week. Even though Chance Bixby, the janitor, had cleaned it up, he had not fixed the hole yet. If only the town council would spend some money on this place, they could restore the mansion to its former glory.

Passing several rows of bookshelves, she counted seven patrons. Miss Penwell's voice played through Callie's mind. *"You should know how many people are in the library at all times."*

Mrs. Anderson looked up from her reading. "Hello, Callie, dear."

Callie smiled and waved at the older woman then moved her cart to the gigantic fireplace. The white limestone hearth had been blackened with soot when the fireplace was used years ago, but now skeletal radiators heated the room in the winter. Those radiators sometimes clicked and hissed alarmingly, making more noise in the library than a group of excited schoolchildren.

Callie selected a book from the cart called *Cowboys of the Old West* and displayed it on the wide mantel. She had just finished it last night. *Such a great read.* No wonder the author, Herbert Dreyfuss, was so famous. Of course, having a weekly syndicated newspaper column that was read all over the nation helped his fame, too.

She glanced at the other volumes on display. Two history books and three fiction, all published years ago. She sighed. If only she could fulfill her dream of owning a bookstore, she could have new books all the time. *And I would read every single one of them.*

Behind the main room, the former dining area had been remodeled as a children's book nook. Callie wheeled her cart through the wide archway. She greeted a young mother with two children who were seated at one of the small tables.

After reshelving a dozen books in the children's section, Callie pushed the empty cart back to the front of the library. On the other side of the mansion through double-wide french doors, she glanced into the conservatory. It ran the width of the house, with tall windows and plants—a comfy place with sofas where people liked to sit and read.

A loud guffaw drew her attention.

She frowned. Bruce MacKinnon and Vern Snyder were making way too much noise. *"You must keep the patrons quiet so others are not disturbed."* Miss Penwell's voice again.

Callie walked into the conservatory, folded her arms, and stared at the two old men. They didn't notice her scowl. It was probably because her glasses, which her sister called "Coke-bottle bottoms," made her eyes look big and round. Tonya said Callie looked like she was always about to say *Huh?*

She did not appreciate her sister's opinion.

Bruce held an open newspaper and pointed to the article he was reading. "Listen to what Herbert Dreyfuss says." His *r*'s rolled slightly. "Wyoming is the best place in the United States to raise kids."

"Now ain't that a hoot?" Vern had a thin, high voice, but it was loud—probably because he seldom wore his hearing aid. "That Dreyfuss is a smart one."

"Aye, that he is."

"He's so famous, and here he says Wyoming, our grand old state, is the best. Too bad his column's only in the paper once a week."

Bruce turned a page. "I enjoyed that article last Friday on the history of golf. Dreyfuss does good research. Made me feel like a boy again, before I left bonny Scotland."

Callie cleared her throat. "Excuse me, but you two need to keep your voices down." She motioned around the conservatory to the other library patrons—ten of them, some sitting on sofas and others studying at tables near the back of the room.

Vern looked at Bruce. "What'd she say?"

"Are you trying to tell us how to live, Callie Brandt?" Bruce spoke in a loud voice. "Why, I remember the day you were born, and here you are, reprimanding me about talking too loud in the library."

Vern laughed. "Shoot! I remember when her daddy was born."

Callie rolled her eyes. "If you want to talk, go upstairs to one of the conference rooms." Several of the bedrooms had been modified into study rooms with soft lighting, tables, and chairs.

"A conference room!" Vern patted the sofa. "But the chairs up there are hard. We want to be comfortable."

"That's the truth." Bruce shook the paper with a rattle. "All right, Callie, we'll be good."

Vern perused his paper. "You won't hear another peep from us."

Callie stood there a moment, but the two men didn't move. Bruce MacKinnon had always reminded her of Clark Gable.

He had a commanding presence and was still a handsome man, even in his seventies. As president of the town council, folks looked up to him.

She walked to the checkout counter, remembering another pet saying from the head librarian. *"I would love this job if it weren't for the people!"*

Callie moved behind the counter and turned her back to look at the reserved books on the shelves. If some of these people didn't pick up their interlibrary loans, she would have to send them back to Casper.

Behind her, a patron placed books on the desk. "I'll be right with you," she said, shoving a reserved book back in place.

"Take your time."

Callie didn't recognize the bass voice. Must belong to that new guy in town. What was his name? It was an unusual name, nothing common like John or Tom. He had visited the library yesterday, and Miss Penwell informed her the man was an insurance salesman.

What is he doing in a little town like Fort Lob? Young people didn't move in—they moved out. The shrinking population, now fewer than five hundred, was predominantly made up of older folks, many retired.

She turned around. "Hello. Thanks for waiting."

He smiled. "Sure."

My goodness, he's handsome! She adjusted her glasses. This was the first time she had seen him up close.

Callie pulled the stack of five books toward her. His library card lay on top, and she glanced at his name before she flashed it under the scanner. *Lane Hutchins.*

While she checked out Lane's books, Callie checked *him* out. He was tall—at least six feet—with brown hair and brown eyes and no glasses to cover his good looks. Nice hands—tanned and clean with trim nails—and no wedding ring.

No wedding ring! Her heart leaped at the implications. But as she slid another book under the scanner's laser, her shoulders drooped. Why should she get her hopes up? Her sister would probably snag him. Tonya just glanced at a man with her beautiful twenty-twenty-vision eyes, batted her thick lashes a few times, and he would ask her out.

Callie pasted a smile on her face, determined to be friendly. "There you go, Mr. Hutchins." She pushed the books across the counter toward him.

"Thank you."

"You're new in town. Didn't you just move here?"

"Uh, yes." He picked up the heavy volumes and stowed them under one arm. "About three days ago."

"I've lived here all my life, except the few years I was in college. The University of Wyoming, of course."

He nodded and moved toward the door.

Callie didn't want him to leave. "Do you have family here in Wyoming?"

He turned. "I grew up in Cheyenne. Have a good day."

"So, where are you staying right now?"

He pulled on the doorknob. "Down the street." The door shut behind him.

Callie frowned. "Down the street" could be anywhere in this small town. He must be renting an apartment at The Stables, Mrs. Wimple's place. Didn't she have an extra one available? Callie would ask her at church on Sunday.

She turned back to the reserved books. Evidently Lane Hutchins was the type who kept to himself. But time would tell why he was here. A person couldn't hide in a small town like Fort Lob, Wyoming.

❧

Lane blew out a breath. *What a nosy girl.* A warm, dry breeze lifted his hair as he walked the four blocks to The Stables.

Why couldn't he move to a small town without people asking questions? He had lived in other small towns, and most people didn't pay any attention to him.

But Fort Lob, Wyoming, was the smallest town he had lived in during the past five years. It was number sixteen in his venture to live in a small town in every state in the Union. The thing that surprised him about this town was its fantastic library. *What a find!*

The rumble of a muffler sounded behind him, and he turned as a black 1972 Ford Mustang thundered by. The kid behind the wheel bopped to loud music. His car backfired twice as he hit the brakes at a stop sign, and when he took off, the Mustang protested with a screech of tires.

Lane shook his head. Had he ever craved that much attention when he was sixteen?

Arriving at his new place, Lane opened the door beside the garage and took the inside stairs two at a time to his second-floor apartment. Mrs. Wimple had informed him that her apartment building used to be a horse stable, built by James Thomas Lob himself in 1878. Now the stables on the first floor formed the garage for the residents' cars, and the rooms upstairs had been divided into apartments.

That's what I like—living history.

In the tiny kitchen, he set his books on the table and looked out the window. From here he could see Main Street, which dead-ended at the imposing Victorian mansion that housed the Dorsey-Smythe Library. The mansion was built on a small hill and towered over Fort Lob. Between the library at one end and the post office at the other, Main Street was lined with shops, including a grocery, a Laundromat, a hardware store, a newspaper office, and two restaurants. The residential streets—with names like Elk, Bison, and Bighorn—spread out from Main.

And that was the extent of Fort Lob, Wyoming.

A smile touched his lips as he thought back to the conversation he overheard in the library's conservatory. Those old men sure liked Herbert Dreyfuss. In fact, everywhere Lane stayed in America, people spoke highly of the author and his articles in the newspaper.

He took a seat at the table and opened one of the books. "People enjoy your writing, Uncle Herb. Especially the old people." He chuckled.

Then his mind drifted to the girl with the curly dark hair who had checked out his books. She certainly asked a lot of questions. But she had a pretty smile, and he liked the way her mouth moved when she talked. She might be attractive if she didn't wear those thick glasses that magnified her eyes.

One of the old men had called her Callie. Callie Brandt. *Pretty name.*

Lane sighed, thinking of the lonely life he led. It was nice to have someone take an interest in him for a change. Maybe he would spend more time at the library. . . .

But no, he should avoid Callie Brandt and her questions. He planned to stay only three months in Fort Lob gathering information, and then he would move on. Hopefully, no one would find out who he really was.

two

Callie stacked the older woman's three books and slid them across the counter. "Two weeks, Mrs. Nielsen. They're due on Saturday, August sixteenth."

"Thank you, dear." She placed the books in her bag and tottered toward the library's entrance. Just as she reached for the handle, the door burst open, and Murray Twichell, dressed in his patrolman uniform, strode inside and almost trampled the woman with his polished black boots.

"Whoa!" Murray caught Mrs. Nielsen's arms before she fell down. "Sorry, Mrs. Nielsen. Didn't mean to run you over."

Callie rushed to the door. "Mrs. Nielsen! Are you okay?"

"Oh, I'm fine, dear." She placed her hand over her heart. "Just startled, that's all."

"I'm so sorry." Murray looked concerned and then seemed to remember he was part of the Wyoming Highway Patrol. He straightened, stretching as tall as his five-foot, six-inch frame would allow him. Placing his left hand over his patrolman's badge and his right hand on the gun holster residing on his hip, he bowed slightly. "I sincerely hope you will accept my most humble apology, ma'am."

"Oh, Murray." Mrs. Nielsen laughed. "I'm all right. Really."

Callie took her elbow. "Let me walk you home."

"No, dear. You have work to do." She exited through the doorway. "No harm done."

Murray closed the door, and a puff of warm air wafted the strong scent of his Stetson aftershave toward Callie. He brushed a hand over his reddish brown crew cut. "Whew!

Every time I come to the library, I run into someone I know. This time I literally ran into someone."

"You need to be more careful, Murray." Callie walked back to the checkout desk, away from his overpowering fragrance. "The last place a person expects to be injured is at a library." She pulled a book from the Reserved shelf. "Your reservation came in from Casper. *A History of Gunfights in America* by Herbert Dreyfuss." She shook her head as she laid the book on the counter. "Well, if that's what you want to read. . ."

"Hey, this is going to be interesting." Murray picked it up. "Have you ever read anything by Dreyfuss?"

"Of course. I've read all his books except this one. It was just published. I'll read it because I love history, but gunfights are not my favorite subject."

"His research is amazing." He pointed the book at her. "When you read history by Herbert Dreyfuss, you know this is not some piece of fiction. It really happened."

"True." She held out her hand. "Your library card, please."

Murray unfastened the brass button on his uniform shirt pocket. "Why do you need my card? You know who I am."

"I know *everyone* in this town, but it's one of Miss Penwell's rules. 'All patrons must present their library card at time of checkout.'"

"Oh, brother." Murray fished the card from his pocket and handed it to her. "By the way, Callie. . ." He lowered his voice. "I have some business over in Lusk this evening. Thought maybe you and me could have dinner and catch a movie." He raised his reddish eyebrows then jiggled them up and down.

Callie looked straight across the counter into his blue eyes. She had always thought Murray Twichell looked like a leprechaun. All he needed was a green suit. "Not this week, Murray, but thanks for asking." She scanned his book.

"Come on, Callie. It's Saturday night. We need an evening in the big city."

In Lusk? "I have to work until six o'clock."

"So? I'll pick you up at six. I'm so busy with my highway duties, you hardly ever see me. When was the last time you saw my handsome face at this library? Three weeks ago?" He placed his right hand over his badge. "My heart yearns within me for time spent alone with you, my darling, and only you."

Callie rolled her eyes. "You've been reading those poetry books again, haven't you?"

"I don't read poetry," he scoffed. "I check those books out for my mother in the nursing home. Now come on, Callie. Let's make it an evening on the town."

She pushed his library card across the counter. Murray Twichell was the only guy who ever asked her out. They had grown up together, and when they were twelve years old, he declared he was going to marry her someday. But Murray was not *the one*, and she was tired of dating him every three or four weeks. "Sorry, not this weekend. I don't. . ."

Her words died as the front door opened and a man walked in. Lane Hutchins? He was here yesterday—and the day before.

Callie smiled. "Hi, Mr. Hutchins. Back at the library so soon?"

"I'm returning these." He set down the five books she had checked out yesterday. "I also need to research something and was wondering if you could help me."

"I'd be glad to." She motioned to Murray. "This is one of Wyoming's patrolmen, Murray Twichell, and—"

"You new in town?" Murray stuck out his hand. He wasn't smiling.

Lane shook hands. "Lane Hutchins. I just moved here a few days ago. I'm staying at The Stables."

So, he does live there.

Murray frowned. "What's your business in Fort Lob, Hutchins? It better be legitimate."

"Murray!" Callie felt like slapping him across the nose. "A person has a right to live in Fort Lob if he wants to, or anywhere else for that matter."

"Just doing my job." Murray stretched to his full height, which still fell short of Lane's by six inches. "The townspeople count on their cops to keep law and order. We don't want any unsavory characters moving in."

"I understand, sir, and my business is quite legitimate." Lane had a serious expression on his handsome face. "People in a small town are protective of their community, and rightly so."

"That's right." Murray looked at Callie. "Smart man." He picked up his book and walked to the door. "Welcome to Fort Lob, Hutchins. See you later, Callie." He exited the library.

Lane turned to Callie. "Was he carrying a Herbert Dreyfuss book?"

"Yes, the new one about gunfights. I had to order it on reserve from the Casper library."

He nodded. "It's only been out a few weeks. I guess you haven't had time to buy a copy for the Dorsey-Smythe Library."

"Well, that's not the problem." Callie looked down, shuffling some papers into a neat pile. It was hard to concentrate with Lane's brown eyes staring at her. "Usually Miss Penwell buys all the bestsellers for our library—in fact, we bought all the other Dreyfuss books—but the town council put a cap on our spending."

"Oh?" Lane folded his arms. "Does that mean you won't be able to buy any new books?"

"That's exactly what it means. They cut our funding, and we haven't bought a new book in four months." She motioned behind her at the thirty or so volumes on reserve. "I have to order books from Casper all the time now. And if they don't have it, I call the library in Cheyenne."

He nodded. "I grew up in Cheyenne with my aunt and uncle, but I've lived in other places more recently."

"Oh." *His aunt and uncle?* Maybe he was an orphan. "So were you—"

"Say, I need your help." He glanced up the wide staircase. "Are your reference books upstairs?"

"Yes, let me show you." She walked to the stairway. "What's your topic?"

"I'm interested in Yellowstone National Park."

Callie ascended the stairs. "In that case, I'll show you the Wyoming Heritage Room. There's lots of information about Yellowstone in there, and unlike the reference books, you can check them out."

"Good." Lane moved up to walk beside her. "I figured a library in Wyoming would carry a number of volumes on Yellowstone, and this is one of the best libraries I've ever visited."

"Thanks to Mildred Dorsey-Smythe." She didn't mention how fast the library was going downhill—thanks to the town council.

They entered the former master bedroom that was packed with shelves of geographical books and local history tomes. Callie scanned the volumes as she walked down the aisles. Lane followed her.

"Here we are." She pointed to four shelves. "Yellowstone National Park. You have a lot to choose from."

"Wow." A spark jumped into his eyes. "This is great."

Callie wished she could stay with him, but her job of pointing out the books was done. "Let me know if you need more help."

"I will." Lane pulled a book from the shelf. "Thanks, Callie." He opened the volume and began perusing it.

Her heart did a little flip as she left the room. *He said my name.* She almost floated down the stairs.

A redheaded blur, in the form of eight-year-old Kincaid Watson, barreled into her as she turned toward the checkout counter. Her daydream disappeared with the impact.

"Sorry, Callie." Kincaid dashed out the front door.

Callie trudged to the desk. Who was she kidding? Lane would never be attracted to her with her ugly glasses. She would probably end up like Miss Penwell, working in the library her whole life as an unmarried librarian. Even if she saved up the resources to begin her dream bookstore, she would do it single-handedly—and single.

But Lane had never answered Murray's question about what he was doing here. Was it to sell insurance? If so, wouldn't he be handing his business card to every patron in the library? On the other hand, the citizens of Fort Lob didn't need an insurance man in town. Everyone got their insurance over the phone through agents in Casper or Cheyenne.

So why did Lane Hutchins move here?

three

At exactly two o'clock, Callie heard the regimented tap of sensible shoes striding toward her. *I could set my watch by her arrival.*

Miss Lucille Penwell marched into the library.

Callie moved to let the head librarian take her place behind the counter. "Good afternoon, Miss Penwell."

The older woman pursed her lips, causing the skin above them to pucker into ripples. Her thin face and high cheekbones made her look like a skeleton, and the short-cropped gray hair did not soften her angular features. "How many reserved books were picked up?"

"Six or seven, I think."

Miss Penwell adjusted her wire-rimmed glasses. "You should know exactly, Miss Brandt. Did you make any phone calls to remind people about their books?" She pressed a few keys on the computer.

"Yes, Miss Penwell."

The head librarian kept her eyes on the computer screen. "And how many patrons are in the building right now?"

Callie had counted five minutes ago, knowing Miss Penwell would ask. "Eight people are in the main room, four children in the book nook, eleven people in the conservatory, and one person upstairs." She wondered how long Lane Hutchins would stay. He had been in the Wyoming Heritage Room almost two hours.

Miss Penwell scanned down the list of those who had checked out. "Only seven books from Casper were picked up.

Why don't these people come and pick up their books? Don't they understand we have to order these from somewhere else? We have to send them back."

Callie shrugged, knowing it was useless to answer.

Outside, a car backfired.

"Oh, that awful Spencer boy is here." Miss Penwell glared at Callie as if it was her fault. "I hope he didn't bring any of his friends with him. The last time they were in the library, they made so much noise that I kicked them out."

Chance Bixby, the janitor, ambled toward the conservatory. He held a mop in one hand, and the front of his shirt was soaked, emphasizing his potbelly. He glanced at the two women and lifted his baseball cap an inch. "Hey there, Callie." The light cast a glint on his gold front tooth.

"Mr. Bixby!" Miss Penwell folded her arms across her thin chest and stared at him.

"Well, hello there, Lucille. Nice day, eh?" He moseyed toward the conservatory.

Miss Penwell huffed out a breath. "A word with you, Mr. Bixby."

He stopped and frowned at her.

"Have you fixed that hole in the ceiling of the main room?"

"No, I haven't." He began to walk away.

"Why not? It's not going to fix itself. That hole is a danger to our library patrons. More plaster could fall and hurt someone."

Oh no. Callie let a sigh escape. Miss Penwell was looking for a fight.

Chance stopped. "No money. That's why."

"What do you mean? We have a repair fund."

"It's empty—as if you didn't know." Chance headed toward the conservatory.

"Mr. Bixby, come back here! I'm not finished speaking with you!"

Chance sighed and walked back to the checkout counter. "Well, I'm done. If there's no money in the repair fund, how can I fix anything? No money, no repair. Even *you* should be able to understand that."

Miss Penwell ignored the insult. "Then talk to the town council—"

"I've talked to them!" His voice increased a decibel. "And they're taking their good old time trying to decide if the library's worth repairing."

"What?" Miss Penwell's gaunt face paled. "Of course it's worth repairing. Use your own money! Plaster can't cost that much."

"My own money?" Chance eyed her. "Do you know the little pittance I make at this job? If I didn't have my pension from the army, I'd be on the street!" He looked at Callie. "You know it's true."

Callie didn't want to get involved in the argument, even though she agreed with Chance. Her librarian's salary was too low to live on by herself, which was why she still lived at home with Mom and Dad.

Chance looked back at Miss Penwell. "You're the head librarian. Maybe *you* should pay for it."

Miss Penwell pursed her lips. "I'm sure the town council will pay you back for—"

"Pay me back? Oh sure." He slapped his hand on the counter. "In five years, they might get around to voting on it."

"What seems to be the problem here?"

The three of them turned toward the voice coming from the conservatory.

Bruce MacKinnon strode up to the checkout counter. "The entire library can hear you two." He kept his voice low. "I suggest you take your fight outside."

Miss Penwell scowled. "We are not fighting. I merely suggested—"

"We are too fighting, Lucille!" Chance thumped his mop handle on the floor as he turned to Bruce. "She's being ridiculous, telling me to use my own money to make repairs. Now where is *that* going to end, I ask you."

Bruce's eyebrows dipped. "But the library has a fund for repairs."

"We have zero money in our fund, Mr. Town Councilman, but a certain town council is too stingy to—"

"Did you put in a request?"

"Yes! Last week! I talked to Ralph Little, since he's the treasurer." Chance shook his head. "Haven't heard a word."

Bruce sighed. "Ralph said nothing to me. But we have a council meeting tonight, and I'll be sure to bring it up. In the meantime. . ." Bruce took his wallet from his back pocket. "Here's some money to buy plaster." He handed Chance a crisp fifty-dollar bill.

Miss Penwell's eyebrows shot up. "Bruce! You shouldn't give him your own money."

"Aha!" Chance waved a thick finger in her face. "He shouldn't spend his money to fix the library, but I can spend mine. Is that it?"

"I never said that."

"That's exactly what you said."

"You are putting words in my mouth!"

"Hold on, you two!" Bruce clapped his hand on Chance's shoulder. "Let's stop this foolishness. Buy the plaster and fix the hole."

Chance nodded and stomped toward the back of the building.

Bruce leaned across the counter. "Now, Lucille, you have to stop these arguments." His voice was low as he took her hand in his. "No one wants to hear you bickering."

Miss Penwell snatched her hand away. "This is *my* library,

and I'll do as I please."

He shrugged. "Suit yourself, Lucille, but someday—someday *soon*—you may discover that someone else is running this library." He glanced at Callie. "And that is the town council speaking."

Miss Penwell's eyes narrowed. "Are you threatening me?"

He cleared his throat. "Guess I'll gallivant over to the Cattlemen's Diner for a good supper. T-bone steak is the Saturday night special." He moved toward the door. "See you later, ladies."

"Good-bye, Bruce." Callie was glad another infamous Chance-Lucille argument was over. They always ended one of two ways: Either Chance would stalk off and Miss Penwell would purse her lips for a half hour, or Bruce MacKinnon would stop it. Callie was caught in the middle—she had to stay on Miss Penwell's good side, but she liked Chance. He was a good janitor, and he was usually right.

She sighed as she stacked books on a cart to reshelve. Catching a movement from the corner of her eye, she glanced toward the stairway. Lane Hutchins descended, a huge stack of books in his arms.

He approached the desk and set the volumes on the counter.

Miss Penwell frowned. "You're checking out all those books?"

He grinned. "I have more." He ran back up the stairs and disappeared around the corner.

"He can't check out all these." Miss Penwell counted the books with her pencil. "He has eleven books here, and he's going to get more?"

Callie winced. Lane was going to catch the wake of Miss Penwell's bad mood. "But we don't have a rule about how many books a person can check out."

"We do for him! This man is a stranger, and who knows

where he came from? My intuitions often prove correct, you know."

No, I didn't know.

Lane descended the stairs with an equally tall stack of books. "This should do it." He set them beside the other books.

"Young man." Miss Penwell pursed her lips. "You may either go upstairs and study these in one of the conference rooms, or you may check out five books."

Callie's mouth dropped open. "Five books? But, Miss Penwell—"

"Miss Brandt!" The head librarian turned her frown on Callie. "You stay out of this. I believe you have some reshelving to do."

Callie folded her arms. *I'm staying right here.*

"Now then." Miss Penwell raised an eyebrow at Lane. "What will it be?"

Lane tapped his fingers on his chin. "I didn't realize I could only check out five." He looked at the two stacks. "Guess I'll take five out and put the rest back." He lifted the top five books from the first pile.

"Good." Miss Penwell looked at the computer. "Your library card." She held out her thin palm.

Lane's eyes met Callie's as he took out his wallet. She shook her head. She wished Bruce MacKinnon was still here to talk some sense into Miss Penwell.

He handed over his card. "I'll take the rest upstairs while you're checking these out."

"And I'll help you." Callie grabbed an armful of books before Miss Penwell could stop her. She marched up the stairs behind Lane.

As they entered the Wyoming room, she glanced around to make sure no one was there. "Lane, I'm so sorry." She looked at the call number on a book spine. "Miss Penwell seems to thrive on being mean."

He put back one of his volumes. "That's one thing I've learned about living in small towns. The townspeople don't trust strangers."

"Miss Penwell doesn't trust anyone!"

"It's okay. I'll come back on Monday and get the information I need."

Callie shelved another book. "If I were you, I'd come in the mornings. Miss Penwell works from two o'clock until the library closes at nine."

"And you work in the mornings?" He leaned against a bookshelf and thrust his hands into his pockets.

Callie gazed at his tall, relaxed stance and closed her mouth to keep in a wistful sigh. "I work from when we open at ten until six at night."

"Six days a week?" He looked concerned.

"We're closed on Wednesdays—and Sundays, of course."

He raised his eyebrows. "Oh, closed on Wednesdays. I'm glad you told me." He smiled at her before moving toward the door. "I guess we should face the music, as the saying goes."

They descended the stairs. Lane took his five books and thanked Miss Penwell for her time. His sweet attitude didn't improve her sour disposition.

Callie watched him walk out the door. She probably wouldn't see him again until Monday morning.

It was a depressing thought.

four

Lane glanced at the vintage sunburst clock on the kitchen wall. Six o'clock. He wasn't fond of the decor in his little yellow and orange kitchen, but it didn't matter. At least the clock worked. What mattered was that it was supper time, and he had nothing to eat.

He had a sudden craving for a frozen dinner—something quick and easy. That was how he defined good food when he had to make it himself. Good thing he brought his microwave. As with most furnished apartments in small towns, that appliance was missing. And a microwave was a necessity for Lane Hutchins.

It took him all of three minutes to walk across Main Street to the grocery store. A bell tinkled overhead as he pushed the door open.

"Hello there!" The man behind the cash register had a booming voice. His barrel-like chest, covered with a white shirt and green grocer apron, had plenty of lung power. "Welcome to Wilkins Grocery."

"Thanks." Lane glanced down the long, narrow aisles that extended all the way to the back of the building. The shelves were crowded with boxes and produce. "Uh, do you have any frozen dinners?"

"Sure thing!" The man nodded his full head of gray hair and moved down one of the aisles.

Lane followed him.

"By the way, the name's Jim Wilkins." He stuck out his meaty hand.

Lane shook it, which was difficult since the man kept walking. "Nice to meet you, Mr. Wilkins. I'm Lane Hutchins."

"Call me Jim. I hear you're new in town."

"Yes, sir. Just moved here a few days ago."

"You'll love Fort Lob. It's a great place to live." At the back wall, Jim stopped at a row of upright freezers with glass doors. "All the frozen stuff is back here. If you need milk, the dairy case is over there to the left against the wall. Help yourself."

"Thanks."

Jim walked to the front of the store as Lane glanced over the frozen dinners. He seemed to be the only customer. Probably everyone was at home eating supper. He picked out three dinners and stowed them under one arm, then he meandered to the dairy case.

The bell over the door jangled.

"Hey there, Callie!" Jim's voice boomed out.

Lane froze.

"Hi, Jim. I need to pick up a gallon of milk and a few other things for Mom before I go home. Be right back."

Yep, that was Callie's voice. *And she's headed straight toward me!* Lane sneaked over to the aisle of canned vegetables, hoping she wouldn't see him.

The dairy case door opened.

This is too close. Lane turned, and his elbow bumped a can of green beans. It fell to the floor with a *thud.*

Callie peered into the vegetable aisle, her magnified eyes widening behind her glasses. "Lane?"

"Oh, uh, hi, Callie." He picked up the can and placed it on the shelf. "Fancy meeting you here."

"Well, it *is* a small town." She glanced at the frozen dinners under his arm. "Are you, um, shopping?"

He shrugged. "Just picking up something to eat tonight."

Her eyebrows lifted. "Well, you know, if you'd like a home-cooked meal, you're welcome to come over to our house. Mom always has plenty of food. She wouldn't mind at all if you popped in."

Just what I need. . . . "Uh, no thanks. I have some work to do tonight."

"Are you sure? My mom's a great cook. One of the best in Fort Lob, in fact."

He chuckled. "Thanks for the offer, but I'd better turn you down." He strode off to the front of the store. "See you later."

"Lane, wait!"

He stopped and turned toward her.

"I was just wondering. . . ." She bit her lip. "Are you going anywhere to church tomorrow?"

"Church?" That was right, tomorrow was Sunday. He hadn't been inside a church since his uncle died. "I don't know of any churches around here, so—"

"Then I'll invite you to ours!" She smiled. "We have a great fellowship, and all the folks are real friendly."

Lane hadn't noticed any churches in the area. "Where is it located?"

"On Bighorn Avenue, two blocks west of here. Turn south on Bighorn and go about a half mile. It's a little white church with a thin steeple. You can't miss it."

He nodded, intrigued again with the way her mouth moved when she spoke. "So there's more to this little town than just the businesses on Main Street?"

Callie huffed out a breath. "Of course! We have three churches, a school—even a jail! Fort Lob is way bigger than it looks."

Lane grinned. "Don't get your dander up, Callie. I was just teasing."

"Oh." She adjusted her glasses. "Well, anyway, our church

service starts at eleven o'clock. Of course, if you want to come to Sunday school at ten, you're more than welcome. My brother teaches the singles' class. We have fifteen members right now—every single adult in the congregation."

Overwhelmed, Lane shook his head. "I'll just go to church maybe. Thanks for the info."

"Hope you can make it. I'll keep an eye out for you."

"Yeah. See you." Lane walked to the cash register. *Church?* He didn't want to go to church, and he wasn't about to go just because Callie invited him. He set down the frozen dinners at the checkout.

"Is this it?" Jim ran the first box over the scanner. "We do have a great church. You should come and meet some of the town folks. You'll enjoy it."

Lane sighed. He should have known that Jim, with the booming voice, would have good hearing, too. And of course, ironically, he would attend the same church as Callie in this little town.

Jim packed the dinners in a grocery sack. "That'll be nine dollars and forty-two cents."

Lane pulled his wallet from his back pocket and handed over a ten-dollar bill.

"We have a great preacher." Jim took the money and opened the cash drawer. "Every Sunday he feeds us with the Word. I've learned more under Pastor Reilly's teaching than any other man of God. A Christian can really grow in our church." He handed Lane his change. "Hope to see you tomorrow."

Lane nodded. "Yeah, thanks." He took the bag, and the bell jingled as he left the store.

Crossing Main Street, he mused over Jim's words. They awakened memories Lane hadn't thought of in seven years. A sudden longing came over him—a longing to hear a good sermon. A longing to get back in fellowship with God.

I think I'll go tomorrow. He could sneak in just as the service was starting and sit in the back. No one would even know he was there.

❧

Callie paced in front of the church building, looking down the road. Where was he? She had spent a half hour in prayer last night, specifically praying that Lane would come to church today. *Oh, Lord, please make him come. Push him, Lord!*

The strains of the organ floated outside, playing the introduction to "All Hail the Power of Jesus' Name." The congregation started singing.

A warm summer breeze blew a strand of hair across her glasses. She brushed it away then smoothed her skirt down with both hands, hoping the wind wouldn't pick it up.

A motorcycle rumbled down the street toward her.

Callie shrank against the building. She didn't like motorcyclists and didn't want this one to see her. She had known a few boys in college who roared through the streets of Laramie on their cycles. They seemed to have a penchant for black leather jackets and earrings.

The motorcycle slowed. The driver wasn't wearing a helmet.

Callie's mouth dropped open. *Lane?*

He pulled into the parking lot across from the church. He wasn't wearing a black leather jacket and earrings; he was wearing a short-sleeved shirt and tie.

He looked *good.*

The congregation was on the third verse as Lane approached the church. He ascended the stairs and stopped short when he saw Callie.

She stepped forward. "Good morning, Lane."

"Callie." He hesitated, a question in his brown eyes. "I

didn't think anyone would be out here. Thought I'd just sneak in the back."

"I was waiting for you, and I'm glad you came." She looked down, suddenly feeling like a love-struck girl in junior high. But it was too late to backtrack. "Would you like to sit with me?"

He shrugged. "Sure. Lead the way."

She opened the door. The congregation was standing, sustaining the last note. She led Lane down the side aisle.

Halfway down, the song leader seated the congregation. The air rustled as they took their seats. Callie saw her parents in the middle of the fourth pew from the front. She slid into place next to Mom. Lane settled beside her.

❧

Lane glanced around, feeling conspicuous. Callie *would* have to sit way up here in the front. The auditorium was crowded, but it was a small room. He estimated there couldn't be more than seventy people in attendance.

A man with stooped shoulders welcomed the crowd. He looked fragile, probably in his sixties, but he had a strong voice.

Callie leaned toward Lane and whispered, "That's Pastor Reilly."

She looked back at the pastor, and Lane took a moment to study her. From this angle, he could see her eyes in profile behind her glasses. They looked like pretty eyes, and her lashes were long. He wished he could see what she looked like without those awful spectacles.

"And I see we have a visitor." Pastor Reilly looked straight at Lane. "Introduce yourself, young man!"

Startled, Lane glanced around. Was he the only visitor?

"Stand up!" Callie whispered.

He stood, restraining the desire to straighten his tie, and looked at the sea of expectant faces. "I'm Lane Hutchins."

"Lane Hutchins," the pastor repeated. "Where are you from?"

"I just moved here from Gridley, Illinois."

"Ah, Illinois! I'm from the Chicago area myself."

Lane nodded and sat down. Fortunately, after a few comments about Chicago, Pastor Reilly moved on to the announcements.

"Illinois?" Callie whispered. She gazed up at him, but as the light reflected off her glasses, he couldn't see her eyes.

He gave her a nod. *What am I doing here?* He wished he had stayed in his apartment. The town of Fort Lob was too tiny for his venture; the people were too nosy. Perhaps he should move to a larger town in Wyoming. Either Pinedale or Lusk, each with a population of fourteen hundred or so, would be better suited for his purposes.

While he was musing, the ushers came forward to collect the offering. As they passed the plates down each row, piano music began—a rendition of "Onward, Christian Soldiers."

Lane glanced at the piano player and drew in a sharp breath. What a beautiful girl!

With dark hair that was fashionably messy, the girl looked to be in her early twenties. She had an oval face with perfect skin and full lips.

She played with passion, concentrating on the music, weaving about on the piano bench. One moment she leaned into the piano, her eyes never leaving the music. The next moment she leaned away, her eyes still glued to the notes. After striking a chord, she would lift her left hand—with manicured red nails—in the air and crash it back down, amazingly, on the right keys. Despite all her theatrics and the fact that the music sounded difficult, she played the piece to perfection.

At the end, the audience gave her an enthusiastic round of applause. Lane joined in.

The girl smiled and nodded at the audience. Her beautiful dark blue eyes glanced around and then stopped at Lane's.

She locked her gaze with his until he looked away.

As the pastor came back to the podium, Lane leaned over to whisper to Callie. "That piano player's really good."

Callie stared straight ahead. "That's my sister, Tonya."

❧

After the service, Callie introduced Lane to Mom and Dad, and Mom invited him over for lunch. For the next twenty minutes, the church people surrounded him, introducing themselves. He shook hands with them, one by one, until his smile began to falter. Callie felt sorry for him.

"Come on, Lane." She pulled him away from old Edna Beazer. That woman would be talking nonstop on her deathbed. "We'll see you later, Edna. Mom invited Lane over for dinner, so we'd better get going."

"Well, my goodness!" The older woman stopped to suck in her dentures. "I was going to invite him myself, but I know your mother is a good cook. She always brings something wonderful to our church potlucks."

Callie nodded, wiping a drop of Mrs. Beazer's spit from her arm. "Maybe some other time." She pulled Lane toward the door.

The church building was empty, and most of the cars had left. But several people were still talking in the parking lot, including Callie's brother, Derek.

She walked down the steps with Lane. "I noticed you were riding a motorcycle."

The church door slammed shut behind them. "Callie! Wait for me!"

Oh no! Callie pivoted at her sister's voice.

Tonya, in her tight knee-length skirt, gracefully descended the stairs. She looked at Lane. "Hi there! I didn't get to meet you earlier. I had to attend a meeting after the service."

Lane smiled and stuck out his hand. "Lane Hutchins."

Callie sighed. He looked entirely too interested.

"I'm Tonya Brandt." She shook his hand, moving closer to him. "I've heard all about you, Lane. You just can't keep a secret in a small town like Fort Lob." She twittered her signature laugh—the one she used for impressing guys.

He grinned. "Great to meet you, Tonya."

Callie noticed they were still shaking hands.

Lane continued. "I enjoyed your piano playing. Not many people can play that well. It sounded like a difficult piece."

"Thank you so much!" Tonya finally released his hand. "I love playing the piano for our church services. It's such a joy."

"Such a joy?" Callie wanted to throw up. Instead she jumped into the conversation. "We'd better get going. Mom invited Lane for dinner."

"Oh, that's wonderful!" Tonya batted her thick, dark lashes. "Why don't I ride over with you, Lane?"

"Well. . ." He glanced down at her skirt.

"He has a motorcycle." Callie turned to Lane. "You can follow our pickup truck. We're riding home with Derek—our brother."

He nodded. "Okay."

Tonya pouted. "Oh, I wish I could ride over with you. We live seven miles east of Fort Lob on Antelope Road. My dad's a sheep rancher."

Lane raised his eyebrows. "Sounds interesting."

Tonya laid her hand on his arm. "I'm glad you're coming over. We'll have all afternoon to get to know each other."

Callie grabbed her by the elbow. "See you there, Lane." She walked with Tonya to Derek's truck while Lane strode to his motorcycle. Tonya climbed into the cab. Callie followed and settled beside her sister. As she closed the passenger door, she felt her opportunity with Lane slamming shut as well.

The thing she feared had come to pass.

five

Ah! The open road.

Lane enjoyed the seven-mile motorcycle ride out to the Brandt family ranch. He followed the pickup as it rattled down the paved two-lane road. They passed a few other houses that were set way back from the road and were usually surrounded by trees. Small groups of cattle munched contentedly on tufts of wild grass. Besides those few signs of civilization, the road cut a path through barren rolling hills dotted with sagebrush.

He could see the three Brandt siblings through the back window of the truck's cab. Tonya sat in the middle, talking nonstop to her brother. Lane had been impressed with Derek Brandt. Taller than Lane, Derek looked to be in his midtwenties, with dark hair the same color as his sisters'. And that Tonya—what a beauty! She reminded Lane of a Hollywood actress, with her perfect facial features and flawless skin.

Derek slowed and turned left onto a narrow blacktopped drive. Lane followed on his cycle, passing under a wrought iron archway with the words THE ROCKING B RANCH in the middle. The driveway was long, possibly five hundred feet, with a row of evergreen trees marching up the left side. Over a small hill, a farmhouse came into view down in the valley. The front porch ran the entire width of the place, with a swing suspended on the left side near the door. Several wicker chairs sat on the opposite side of the porch. It would be nice to sit there in the shade, sipping a tall glass of lemonade.

The pickup stopped beside the house, and Lane parked

his motorcycle behind it. He had barely dismounted before Tonya appeared at his side.

"Come into the house, Lane. I'm sure Mom has the meal all ready. She's made a beef roast today. I know it will be great, and her mashed potatoes are to die for."

"Sounds good." He gazed into her eyes—those dark blue eyes surrounded by thick black lashes. Definitely Hollywood material.

They ascended the porch steps together. Jake Brandt, Tonya's father, held the door open for them. Like his son, he was tall. He wore glasses, but unlike Callie's, the glasses didn't magnify his eyes.

"Welcome to The Rocking B!" Jake shook his hand. "Come on in."

"Thanks." Lane motioned for Tonya to precede him into the house. As he walked in, the savory aroma of roast beef surrounded him. "Boy! That smells delicious."

"Doesn't it, though?" Tonya agreed. "I'm starving."

Lane followed her into a spacious living room. They passed a pink-flowered sofa sprinkled with pillows, and an upright piano with framed pictures on the top. In the dining room, a large oak table was set with six green and tan place settings. Several steaming bowls of food made his mouth water.

Mrs. Brandt came out from the kitchen. "We're all ready to eat. Hi, Lane. Welcome to our home."

"Thanks." He smiled, trying to remember her first name. "The food smells great." He could see where Tonya got her beauty. Even though Mrs. Brandt looked in her midfifties, she still had a beautiful face. Just like Tonya's, her eyes were dark blue with thick, dark lashes.

"Have a seat, Lane." Jake motioned to the chair on his left as he took the seat at the head of the table.

Tonya slipped into the chair across from Lane. "It's going

to taste as good as it smells. This is a feast fit for a king." She twittered a little laugh.

He smiled. This promised to be an enjoyable meal just because he could drink in her beauty. A saying from Uncle Herb popped into his mind. *"Marry a pretty gal, Lane. You'll have to look at her across the table every morning."*

Mrs. Brandt took a seat at the other end of the table while Derek sat down next to Tonya. Callie slid into the seat beside Lane. Jake asked the blessing, and they passed the food. The next twenty minutes were filled with pleasant conversation and fine dining.

It had been years since Lane had enjoyed such a good home-cooked meal, probably not since he had eaten Aunt Betty's cooking. And she had died ten years ago, when Lane was nineteen. He took second helpings of everything and was actually full. That hadn't happened in a long time, either.

He glanced at his hostess. "That was a delicious meal, Mrs. Brandt."

"Thank you, Lane, but please call me Yvette. Everyone does."

He nodded. "Yvette."

Across the table, Tonya leaned forward. "I hope you liked the homemade rolls."

"Homemade?" He raised his eyebrows. "They were fantastic. I've never tasted such good dinner rolls."

She sat back. "I made them—from scratch, of course."

"So, you have cooking talent as well as musical talent."

Her beautiful eyes widened. "Oh, I have a lot of talents. Not only can I cook and play the piano, I'm also artistic, I love to sew, I'm athletic, and I'm a hairstylist, too. I work at The Beauty Spot over on Elk Road."

"Really?" He grinned, teasing. "Is there anything you can't do?" Lane expected her to lower her beautiful eyes in modesty.

Instead, she looked thoughtful. "Not really. I can do almost anything."

Derek folded his arms. "She's especially good at boasting."

"I am not!" Tonya frowned at her brother.

Derek shrugged. "Then what do you call it?"

Yvette scooted her chair back. "Now, you two. Don't get into an argument. We have company today." She stood. "Girls, help me clear the table, and then we'll have dessert."

Callie stood, and a sigh escaped her lips.

Lane wondered if she was living in Tonya's beautiful shadow. "Do you only have two siblings, Callie?"

She turned toward him. "Actually there are six of us, and I'm in the middle."

"Yep." Jake laid his napkin beside his plate. "We have two married children. Ryan lives in Denver with his wife and sons, and Melissa lives in Colorado Springs with her husband."

Tonya picked up Derek's plate. "Melissa just got married last summer. I fixed her hair, and she looked absolutely gorgeous at her wedding. Molly is her identical twin, and she's a nurse. She works at the Pine River Nursing Home in Douglas."

Lane leaned back as Callie took his plate. "So Ryan is the oldest sibling?" He looked at Jake, but Tonya answered.

"Yes, he's thirty-one." She set down her dishes and counted off her fingers. "It's Ryan, Molly and Melissa, Callie, Derek, and me. I just turned twenty-three last week." She shrugged slightly as she gave Lane a little smile. "I'm the baby of the family."

Jake adjusted his glasses. "I wish my three oldest hadn't moved away. Seems all the young people leave Fort Lob sooner or later, and I don't understand it."

"Well, duh!" Tonya picked up her stack of dishes again. "Fort Lob, Wyoming, is not exactly the hot spot of America, Dad."

He grinned at his daughter. "It gets pretty hot in the summer. Near a hundred degrees most days in July."

She looked at Lane and then rolled her eyes. "That's not what I mean." She giggled as she grabbed some silverware. "I like Fort Lob. I'll probably spend my life here, married to a wonderful man someday." She paused to give Lane a significant look. "But if my husband wants to leave, I'd have to leave, too." She glanced at her dad. "That's just the way it is."

Callie came back from the kitchen and picked up several more dishes.

Lane glanced at her as she took the potato dish from the table. "How long have you worked at the Dorsey-Smythe Library?"

"I got the job right after college graduation four years ago."

"Do you like working there?"

Callie nodded. "I love it. I've always loved to read and—"

"Which is why she wears glasses," Tonya put in. "When the rest of us kids were playing, Callie was sitting in some secluded corner with a book. Absolutely ruined her eyes." Toting her dirty dishes, she walked to the kitchen.

Lane was glad she was gone. His infatuation with Tonya faded the more she talked. "Tell me about the library, Callie. With a name like the Henry Dorsey-Smythe Memorial Library, it must have quite a history behind it."

"It does." Setting the dishes down, she took her seat beside him. "The history goes back to James Thomas Lob, the founder of our town. For several years in the 1800s, he was a scout for settlers who moved west. But scouting was dangerous work."

Derek leaned back in his chair. "But James Lob wasn't of the same caliber as Kit Carson or Buffalo Bill or Jim Bridger. He never made a name for himself like those other guys."

"I always admired Buffalo Bill Cody," Jake put in. "He was a fascinating man. When the US Army was fighting the Indians, he'd hunt buffalo so they'd have something to eat.

That's how he got his nickname."

"Not the army, Dad," Callie said. "He supplied buffalo meat for the men who were building the transcontinental railroad."

Lane didn't want to get off the subject. "So Lob quit scouting and built this town?"

Callie nodded. "But it wasn't much of a town when he was living."

Jake laughed. "It was more like a few buildings with a big fence around them to keep out the Indians."

"Where does Henry Dorsey-Smythe come in?"

Tonya walked back into the room. "Okay, everyone. Mom is ready to cut the pies." She looked at Lane. "Do you want cherry or apple?"

"Uh. . .cherry would be great."

Tonya smiled. "Whipped cream?"

"Sure." Lane smiled back.

Tonya gazed at him another moment before she took the other orders.

Lane drummed his fingers on the table. As soon as he ate his pie, he would make some excuse to leave. Tomorrow he could ask Callie at the library about the history of Fort Lob. He wondered if there were any books about its founder. Fort Lob seemed to be one of those overlooked towns in the United States with a fascinating history.

On a more personal note, he had to think of some way to get Callie to remove her glasses. She might be as beautiful as her sister.

And a lot less suffocating.

six

On Monday morning, Callie reached beneath the library's checkout desk and pulled out a book to read. Business had been slow this morning. Only twelve people had entered the library, and ten had left. Of the two remaining people, Mrs. Anderson had settled in the conservatory. The other person was Cheyenne Wilkins, Callie's best friend since first grade. Cheyenne worked at the post office, but Monday was her day off.

Removing the bookmark from *Hearts Joined Together*, Callie began reading. This was a new romance novel she had ordered from Casper, and she was already in chapter nine. In a few minutes, she was deep into the story, but every time the library's front door opened, she looked up and noted who came in and who left. After a half hour, she had tallied seven people who had come and gone. Somehow she kept her mind on her book.

"Morning, Callie." Lane Hutchins closed the door and walked toward her.

"Oh!" She shoved the novel under the desk, not bothering with the bookmark, and hoped Lane hadn't noticed the title. She didn't want him to think she was interested in romance.

The sleeves of his blue denim shirt were rolled up to his elbows, and he held two hardcover books in one hand.

"Uh, hi, Lane. I guess you're back to finish your research on Yellowstone."

"Yeah, I should work on that." He laid the two volumes on the desk. "I went down to Cheyenne this morning and got a couple books for the library."

Callie looked at them—two new copies of *A History of Gunfights in America* by Herbert Dreyfuss. "Wow! These are expensive!" He must have bought them at a bookstore, and the retail price was $27.99 each.

He grinned. "It was nothing. Since the town council put a limit on the library's spending, I thought I'd donate these. At least the library will have two new books in its possession."

"Thank you, this is great. I'll have to catalog them." She hoped Miss Penwell would show more favor to Lane for his generous donation. Hmm. . .maybe that was why he bought them in the first place.

Lane folded his arms on the desk and leaned forward. "I'd like to learn more about the history of Fort Lob and this library. Are there any books on the subject?"

"A few." Callie found it hard to breathe with Lane this close. His muscled arms rested on the counter, and she stared at them. "Uh, there are some books in the Wyoming room upstairs, and we also have information on the Dorsey-Smythe family on the third floor."

"The third floor?" Lane stood up straight. "I didn't realize you had a reference room up there."

"We don't." Callie dropped her voice. "It's not open to the public. But if you're interested in the history of the library, we have some old documents, letters, and photographs."

His eyes opened wide. "I'd love to see those."

She glanced around. "Let me make sure no one needs me."

Cheyenne walked in from the conservatory. The green and orange broomstick skirt she wore swirled around her sandaled feet. "Are you busy, girlfriend?" She laid four books on the desk. "I want to check these out."

Callie had always thought Cheyenne was pretty with her blond hair and blue eyes, and her round face sported two deep dimples. Her dad called her "pleasingly plump," but

Cheyenne moaned that she was fat.

"Hi, Lane." Cheyenne's eyes were almost level with his. "Nice to see you again."

"Uh, hi." His brow furrowed.

Callie motioned to her friend. "This is Cheyenne Wilkins. You met her yesterday at church. Her dad owns the grocery store."

"Oh yeah." Recognition dawned on his face. "I think I met the whole town yesterday. So, Cheyenne. . .were you named after the city?"

"Yeah, my mom liked the name. Of course, there was hippie blood in her family, so she had to name me something different." She laughed.

"You're looking rather *hip* yourself today." Callie pointed to Cheyenne's big hoop earrings and the psychedelic headband surrounding her blond hair. Topping her skirt, she wore a neon orange T-shirt.

Cheyenne laughed. "Last night I was cleaning out Mom's old sewing room and found a whole bunch of hippie stuff." She touched the headband. "This belonged to my aunt Vera. She was totally immersed in the hippie culture in the sixties."

Picking up the first of Cheyenne's books, Callie ran it under the scanner. Lane stood at the corner of the desk, perusing the cover of *A History of Gunfights in America*.

Callie picked up Cheyenne's second book. "I'll check these out and then take you upstairs, Lane. Today has been quiet, so I should have plenty of time to show you some things."

As if to prove her wrong, the door burst open and two moms with a passel of kids trooped in. The noise level rose ten decibels. They greeted Callie and Cheyenne. Right behind them, five teen girls walked in and ascended the stairs.

Callie's heart sank. "I'd better stick around the desk for a while, Lane. I'm the only librarian, so—"

"I'll watch the desk for you." Cheyenne turned to Lane. "I used to work here during high school. It'll be fun to check out books again."

Callie cocked her head toward the noisy children's section. "Do you think you can handle all the ragamuffins? Sometimes they check out lots of books."

"Sure." Cheyenne walked behind the desk. "Piece of cake."

"Okay, I'll try to hurry." Callie looked at Lane. "Follow me."

❧

Lane trailed behind Callie, his heart picking up its pace. *Herbert Dreyfuss might get a book out of this research.*

She led him up to the second floor then unlocked a door that held a sign reading EMPLOYEES ONLY. Another set of stairs took them to the third floor, where Callie opened a door into a small room with a slanted ceiling.

"It's warm up here." Lane walked to the window and looked out over the town of Fort Lob. "What a great view!"

"You can see for miles." Callie walked around old furniture, covered with sheets, and stopped in front of a cabinet with glass doors. She took a set of keys from her jeans pocket and unlocked it. Pulling out a large box, she set it on a nearby table. "These are old town documents and photos." She took another box from the cabinet and glanced at a label on the top. "These are letters written by the Lobs and Dorsey-Smythes."

"True history." A thrill ran through him as he opened the lid of the first box. Neatly packed inside were thick envelopes, yellowed with age, and old sepia photographs of Fort Lob in the early 1900s. "Wow, what a gold mine."

Callie went back to the cabinet, and Lane wondered what else that cabinet held. His gaze swung around, and he pointed to three trunks sitting on the floor. "What's in those trunks, Callie?"

"Those belonged to Mildred Dorsey-Smythe. She was the

granddaughter of James Thomas Lob."

"And who was Henry Dorsey-Smythe?"

"Mildred's father. She turned the house into a library and named it after him. She felt her father never got any recognition in this town since her grandfather was so famous."

Lane nodded. When Callie left, he would take a look in those trunks. They might hold some valuable stuff. "When did Mildred die?"

"Almost fifty years ago. And let me tell you, Lane, this house is falling apart. I wish the town council would do something about it."

"Don't they have money to repair it?"

"They have money." She pulled another box from the cabinet then locked it and faced him. "But they *want* it to fall apart. Mildred willed the house to the town to use as a library, and according to her will, it must remain a library unless the town can't keep it in repair." She huffed out a breath. "I think the town council wants to condemn this place."

Fascinating. Lane watched Callie's mouth move as she talked, hardly hearing a word she said. But he heard enough. "This is a great library. I don't know why they want to get rid of it."

"They don't want to get rid of the library itself, but some of the townspeople think the mansion is an eyesore. They want to tear it down and build a modern building."

He nodded. "Progress, I suppose. Some people have no use for living history."

"I know. I've always loved this old house, and I love history."

"Me, too." He gazed at Callie, wishing he could see what was under that pair of glasses. What if she had a beautiful face like her sister? He liked her personality.

With a sigh, he turned to the table. "Is there a chair around here? I'd like to read these documents."

❧

Callie checked out Mrs. Anderson's books and watched as she walked out the door. "We sure have been busy for a Monday."

"I'm glad I was here to help." Cheyenne perched on the stool behind the desk, pulling the edge of her orange T-shirt over her skirt. "You need more librarians, girl. Why doesn't the town council hire more people?"

"That's Miss Penwell's fault. She wants to be in control." Callie sighed. "I do wish I could get away sometimes. I love this place, but I live here for eight hours every day. Even though I get a lunch break, Miss Penwell makes me stay in the library. Sometimes I feel chained to this job."

"Well, I'm going to help you—at least on Mondays. You should get out of the building for an hour."

Lane walked up to the checkout counter. "I agree."

"Oh! Uh, hi, Lane." Callie felt her face heat up. How much had he overheard? "Are you finished on the third floor?"

"No, but I needed a break." He glanced at his watch. "It's twelve thirty, and I feel. . .chained to the library." He grinned. "Why don't I take you out to lunch, Callie? We can visit that diner on Main Street."

Is he asking me out? A quiet excitement filled Callie, but at the same time, she knew she couldn't leave the premises. "I'd love to go with you, Lane, but I have to watch the desk here. My lunch break doesn't start until two, when Miss Penwell arrives."

Cheyenne studied Lane for a moment before her eyes cut to Callie. "Cool idea." She turned her back to Lane and winked at Callie. "You definitely need a break."

Callie opened her mouth, but Cheyenne turned toward Lane and continued. "But you shouldn't take her to the Cattlemen's Diner, Lane—or anywhere else on Main Street, for that matter—unless you want all the locals to listen to your conversation and gossip about you."

He raised an eyebrow. "That bad, huh?"

Cheyenne flipped her blond hair behind her shoulder. "Oh, the gossips in this town are notorious. I could name several in our Main Street eating establishments, but I wouldn't want it to get back to them." She grinned.

"Okay, then. Where could we go for lunch?"

"I've got it!" Cheyenne slapped her hand on the desk. "Why don't you two go to Ray's?"

"Is that a restaurant?" Lane asked.

"Yep. Ray's Burger Retreat. It's a little hamburger place on Rattlesnake Road."

His lips parted. "Rattlesnake?"

Cheyenne laughed. "I never thought of it being located on Rattlesnake—that doesn't sound too appetizing, does it? But Ray has the best burgers around."

Callie placed a restraining hand on Cheyenne's arm. "Listen, I appreciate this, but I can't leave. I'm the only librarian—"

"Now, Callie." Cheyenne folded her arms. "We were just talking about that. Let me watch the library for you. I'm having the time of my life."

"Cheyenne. . ." Callie raised her hands then let them drop. "Your life must be totally boring."

Cheyenne ignored her. "You *know* you want a hamburger. Do something daring for once in your life."

Callie bit her lip. "Well, just so Miss Penwell doesn't find out."

"Who's going to tell her?" Cheyenne laid her hand on Callie's shoulder. "Take a break, girl. Remember how the old song goes. . ." She began to sing softly. "You deserve a break today, so get up and get away. . .to Ray's."

Lane grinned. "Is that how it goes?"

"Well, at least it rhymes. Now shoo!" Cheyenne waved her hand toward the door. "I can hold down the fort for an hour."

Callie breathed a sigh. "Thanks, Cheyenne. I owe you one."

"Oh, you'll owe me more than one."

Lane opened the door for her, and they walked outside. "Do you want to ride on my motorcycle, or do you have a car?"

"Well. . ." Callie pondered as they walked around the library to the back parking lot. She had never liked motorcycles. In fact, the fatalities on motorcycles were high in Wyoming. But Cheyenne's words whizzed through her mind. *"Do something daring for once in your life."* "Um, let's take your motorcycle. That sounds fun." She was glad she was wearing jeans.

When she saw the huge motorcycle with HARLEY-DAVIDSON printed on the side, Callie took a deep breath and prayed for safety.

Lane straddled the bike and motioned to her. "Hop on. You can hang on to me if you want."

Callie managed to get on behind Lane, throwing her arms around his waist as he started the motorcycle. The powerful engine roared to life.

She tightened her grip, feeling his solid muscles beneath her arms.

He looked back at her with a grin. "You're not scared, are you?" he yelled.

"Um, not too much."

He laughed. "Don't worry, just lean when I lean, okay?" Not waiting for an answer, he squeezed something on the left handle, twisted the right handle, and they roared out of the parking lot and down Main Street.

A thrill raced through Callie as she hung on, trying to lean with him. Then reality hit.

I'm going on a date with Lane Hutchins!

seven

Lane drove his Harley down the main street of Fort Lob, relishing the feel of Callie's arms around his waist. Neither wore a helmet, and he could imagine Callie's dark hair flying out behind her. *I want to get to know this girl.* Something about her attracted him. Must be the way her mouth moved. On the other hand, spending Sunday with the Brandt family made him realize how lonely he was.

When they arrived at Ray's Burger Retreat, he parked the bike and helped Callie dismount. He thought of how nervous she had looked when she got on. "You okay?" he asked.

She grinned. "That was fun. But I can't imagine riding all the way down to Cheyenne on this thing. It must get tiring."

"It does." They walked toward the small restaurant building that had huge plate glass windows on either side of the door. "I always wear my helmet when I get on the freeway, and that gets hot. So I'm hot and tired by the time I get to Cheyenne." He opened the door for her.

Callie introduced him to everyone in the restaurant, including Ray, who was surprisingly thin for being a chef, and the waitress named Beverly—a dowdy, middle-aged woman who wore rubber-soled shoes. He even met a dozen customers who were eating lunch. Lane shook hands all around. *You'd think we were at a family reunion.*

They finally settled at a corner booth and ordered the hamburger special. Beverly brought their drink order to the table and left.

For a few minutes, Callie talked about the motorcycle

ride. "I always thought motorcycles were so dangerous. Only daredevils rode them."

He grinned. "Do I look like a daredevil?"

"Definitely not!" She smiled as she played with her straw paper. "I suppose it's a cheap form of transportation, although I can't believe what a huge motorcycle you have. It must have cost you a pretty penny."

He shrugged. "I wanted to get those saddlebags in the back for traveling, so I needed a bigger bike." Lane took a sip of his iced tea. He didn't tell her he had two cars, a Lexus and a Mazda, parked in his garage in Cheyenne. "What I can't believe is how you know everyone in this town." He nodded at the other customers.

Callie raised her eyebrows. "That's what happens when you grow up in a small place. But you said you grew up in Cheyenne with your aunt and uncle. Are you an orphan?"

He nodded. "My parents were killed in a plane crash when I was six years old."

"Oh, Lane." Callie knit her brows. "I'm so sorry to hear that. Do your aunt and uncle still live in Cheyenne?"

"No, both of them are dead now." He didn't want to talk about his past. She might start asking questions that he didn't want to answer. "Tell me about yourself, Callie. Do you have any hopes and dreams for the future?"

A tiny smile tugged at her lips. "I do have a dream, but I've never told anyone about it."

Beverly, holding two large platters, approached their table. "Here's your order." She set a plate in front of each of them. "The mustard and ketchup are right there on the table. Do you need anything else?"

"This should do it for me." Lane glanced at the thick hamburger stacked with lettuce, onions, and tomato slices. "Smells delicious."

Callie nodded. "Thanks, Beverly." As soon as the waitress left, Callie leaned across the table. "Lane? Would you mind saying grace for us?"

Grace? He hadn't prayed over his food in seven years. He cleared his throat. "Sure."

She bowed her head.

He looked down at his plate. "Uh, Lord, thank You for this food." He kept his voice low, almost to a mumble. "Bless it to our bodies. Amen."

"Amen," Callie echoed. She took her napkin and placed it in her lap then grabbed the ketchup bottle.

Lane picked up the mustard, wondering what she thought of his prayer. At the family dinner yesterday, her dad had prayed for seven or eight minutes. Lane thought the man would never stop, but at the same time, Jake Brandt seemed to know God personally—the way Lane used to.

But he didn't want to think about his spiritual problems. The safest thing to do was change the subject. "So, Callie, what's this dream you have?"

She picked up her knife and cut her hamburger in half. "Well, I love to read, as you know, and I've always wanted to—" She glanced around and lowered her voice. "I've always wanted to have my own bookstore. It's been my desire for years, and I've been saving up to rent a storefront in town."

"That's great." He smiled at her. "Dream big, Callie."

She shrugged. "I don't know if it will happen, but I feel in my heart that it's the Lord's will. I already know what the name of my bookstore will be, and the idea came straight from the Lord, too." She leaned forward, and the light from the window reflected off her glasses. "For the Love of Books. That's the name of it." She sat back. "It's an acronym."

"An acronym?"

"Think about it." She smiled, biting her bottom lip at the same time.

"For the Love of Books." Lane pronounced it slowly. "Oh. *Ft. Lob.* That's cool."

With a nod, she picked up her hamburger. "I'm especially interested in history. I'd like to sell books about Wyoming. Our state has such a fascinating past—the scouts and trailblazers, the battles between the army and the Indians, the Oregon Trail, the Pony Express, the transcontinental railroad. . . ."

He laughed. "You're a walking encyclopedia."

Her face tinged pink, and she took a bite of her hamburger.

For the next few minutes, they ate in silence. As Lane chewed on his burger, he also chewed on what Callie wanted to do. He wished he could help her. But a bookstore in Fort Lob? Would she have enough customers?

He set his half-eaten hamburger on the plate. "You know, Callie, I'm wondering if you should tweak your dream a bit."

She frowned. "What do you mean?"

"I like the bookstore idea, but I think you should expand it to include a museum."

"A museum? But Wyoming has lots of museums."

"Not about James Thomas Lob." He leaned forward. "Look at all that stuff in the library. It's just sitting there, collecting dust. You could bring it to life, Callie."

He noticed a shiver run over her. "I would love to do that."

"You could set up a museum and sell Wyoming books in the gift shop." He shrugged. "You'd still have your bookstore."

"That would be a fantastic project—if I could save enough money." She shook her head. "But that might be too big of a dream for me."

❧

I can't afford a museum!

Callie sighed under her breath. She wasn't sure she could

afford a bookstore. But a museum would have to be housed in a building by itself on its own property, and she didn't have that kind of money. Then she'd have to get permission from the town council since Fort Lob owned all those things in the library, and she didn't want a job where she would be accountable to them.

Beverly came to their table. "How about some dessert? Our special today is hot peach cobbler with a scoop of ice cream."

Callie shook her head. "I'm so full, I can't—"

"How about just the ice cream, in a cone?" Lane raised his eyebrows at Callie then turned to Beverly. "We'll take two cones. A large vanilla for me."

They both looked at Callie.

"Uh, okay. I'll take a chocolate cone—small."

Beverly nodded. "One large vanilla and one small chocolate. Be right back."

While they waited, Lane waxed eloquent about the museum. He talked about the photos of the town, the family's history, the old furniture. Callie listened, resting her chin in her hand and enjoying his enthusiasm. Enjoying *him*. But at the same time, she knew the museum idea would never happen. That was certainly a pipe dream, if ever there was one.

Beverly came back with their cones and left.

Lane took a few licks. "This is really good ice cream."

"Ray makes his own. He's famous for it, actually." Callie took a bite and adjusted her glasses. "This has been a wonderful break, Lane." Spending time with Lane and getting to know him was the best part.

"My pleasure." He licked his ice cream into a point. "Like Cheyenne said, you deserved a break." He leaned across the table and lowered his voice. "You needed to rest those eyes."

Lane poked the point of his ice cream at her glasses.

Suddenly she saw nothing through the left lens but a big white spot.

"Hey!" She whipped them off and glanced at the damage before looking up at him. "You did that on purpose."

He grinned. "Yep. Just wanted to see your pretty face." His smile faded. "And you are pretty, Callie—even prettier than I thought."

Heat rose in her face. She wasn't sure if she should thank him for the compliment or yell at him for smudging her glasses. But even though he was blurry and out of focus, the look he gave her as their eyes met stopped her heart and stilled her tongue.

Flustered, she glanced around. "I need something to clean my glasses, but. . ." She scooted to the end of the booth. "Guess I'll have to go to the ladies' room."

"Wait!" Lane held out his hand. "Give them to me. I messed them up; I should fix them."

Callie handed her glasses over. Lane looked at the splotch of ice cream residing on the left lens and pulled a napkin from the holder at the end of the table.

"No, Lane, don't use a napkin. Paper will scratch the lens. I'll ask Beverly to get us—"

"Don't bother." He swiped his thumb across the glass, smearing the ice cream. "I'll just mess it up good, and we'll clean it later." He grinned as he dropped her glasses into his shirt pocket.

She raised her eyebrows. "You're not giving them back?"

"Not yet." Lane folded his arms on the table and leaned toward her. "Why don't you get contacts? You have such pretty eyes, and those glasses are hiding your beauty."

She drew in a surprised breath. Did he say *"beauty"*?

A warm feeling stirred inside Callie. No one had ever told her that before, especially not a handsome single guy like Lane Hutchins. She leaned across the table toward him. "Well, I, uh. . ." She gazed into his eyes.

He gazed back.

Finally she blinked. Several times. "Um. . .what was the question?"

He cleared his throat and sat back. "Contacts? For your eyes?"

"Oh yeah, contacts." Looking down, she sighed. "My eye doctor said they wouldn't work for me."

"So you're stuck with glasses forever?" Lane did not look happy.

"Not necessarily." She shrugged. "Although I might as well be stuck. He said laser eye surgery would work and I could have twenty-twenty vision, but my medical insurance won't pay for it."

Beverly came by the table. "Here's your bill. Well, my goodness, Callie. I've never seen you without your glasses. Don't you look pretty." She picked up their plates. "I never realized how much you look like Tonya."

As she left, Lane winked at Callie. "I was thinking the same thing. But you're even prettier."

Did he say "*prettier*"? Feeling warmth rise in her face, she squinted at her watch. "Oh no! It's after one thirty. Cheyenne is going to have my head."

"I doubt that." Lane stood, took out his wallet, and threw a couple of bills on the table. "She seemed to be enjoying her stint as librarian."

They walked out the door and straddled Lane's motorcycle.

"Are you going to give my glasses back?" Callie circled her arms around his waist.

"Maybe. Someday." He started the cycle, and it thundered to life.

They flew down Rattlesnake Road. Callie held on to Lane

tightly, loving the feel of the wind blowing her hair back. And now it fluttered against her eyelashes. Her heart gave a happy leap. Lane thought she was pretty, even prettier than her sister.

Oh Lord, she prayed, *please let something good come from this.* Did she dare pray that Lane would want to marry her?

But was he a Christian? She just assumed he was, but his prayer for the food didn't give her any confidence about his relationship with God.

Lane slowed down to turn onto Main Street, and Callie smiled at the tall spots of color on the sidewalk who waved to her, even though she wasn't sure who those people were. The entire population of Fort Lob was probably gossiping about them. After all, a person could hardly sneak through town on a motorcycle, especially on Main Street.

When they arrived at the library, Lane pulled up before the door. "I'll drop you off here, and you can let Cheyenne leave."

Callie dismounted. "*Now* will you give my glasses back?"

He gazed at her eyes a moment before he winked. "Not yet." Revving the motor, he guided the cycle to the back parking lot.

Callie laughed out loud as she walked up the library steps using the handrail as a guide and pulled open the front door. She stepped inside, and her smile froze.

The navy blue blob standing behind the checkout desk couldn't be Cheyenne. For one thing, Cheyenne had been wearing an orange T-shirt, and for another thing, this blob was as thin as a skeleton.

"Miss Brandt!" Miss Penwell's voice rang out across the entryway, grating on Callie's nerves. "Where in the world have you been?"

Even without her glasses, Callie knew Miss Penwell's lips were pursed.

eight

Lane jogged up the library steps. Callie's glasses jiggled in his shirt pocket, and he smiled. *She doesn't even realize how pretty she is.* He reached for the library's door handle. How could he give Callie the money for laser eye surgery without offending her? It couldn't be that expensive, probably a few thousand dollars. *I'll think of something.*

He stepped inside and stopped short.

"I should have you fired!" Miss Penwell's arms were folded against her thin chest.

Callie stood in front of the checkout counter, her head bowed.

"You are not to leave this building during your shift, Miss Brandt, and you know that."

Lane strode up to the desk. "Now just a minute." He kept his voice low.

"You!" Miss Penwell's gray eyes widened. "You are the reason! It's because of you that Miss Brandt is in trouble. She knows better than to leave the premises, and you were the devil's agent to cause her to—"

"Listen!" Lane held up both hands, feeling his ire rise. He glanced at Callie's profile. Her head was still bowed, her face pale. Obviously she wasn't going to defend herself.

He took a deep breath. "Miss Penwell, we need to discuss this calmly, like three rational human beings."

"There is nothing to discuss. You dragged my employee to Ray's—"

"All right, Miss Penwell, I apologize. This whole thing was

my fault. Please don't fire Callie over it."

Callie looked up at him. "Lane—"

"No, Callie. I shouldn't have asked you to leave your job." He glanced at Miss Penwell, noting that her lips were pressed together. "It won't happen again; you have my word on that."

"No, it won't happen, young man, because you will not set foot in my library again. I forbid you to come here. No more books for you. I won't have my employees—" She stopped as two older men walked up to the desk. "Bruce! Vern." She frowned. "How long have you two been standing there?"

Lane recognized the men who had liked the article by Herbert Dreyfuss the first time he had seen Callie. *I hope they're on my side.*

The more dignified man, the one from Scotland, stepped forward. "We've been here all afternoon, Lucille. We heard you dismiss Cheyenne—"

"The whole library heard you." The other man pointed to his hearing aid. "Even me."

Callie winced.

The Scottish man drummed his fingers on the desk. "Lucille, I've already discussed this issue with you."

"What issue?" Miss Penwell frowned at him. "As I recall, Bruce, I have never had to deal with an errant employee who left the premises because some boy—"

"Lucille." Bruce lowered his voice as he leaned toward her. "I'm talking about your temper. You cannot prohibit people from using the library." He motioned toward Lane. "And this is not the first time I've heard you doing that. The town council discussed your behavior at our last—"

"My behavior! Why, Bruce MacKinnon! How dare you say that my behavior is anything but outstanding? In fact, exemplary. I've been running this library for thirty-nine years."

The other man spoke up. "And the council thinks it's time you retire."

"Vern, I'll handle this." Bruce turned to Miss Penwell.

"Retire?" Miss Penwell's voice rose with her words. "And just what would I do if I retired? Sit around my house twiddling my thumbs?"

Bruce sighed. "Lucille, you're seventy-two years old—"

"I am not!"

He raised his eyebrows. "You're the same age as me."

Miss Penwell pursed her lips before she spoke. "I'm seventy-one."

"Okay, seventy-one."

"And I'm in excellent health. Excellent, I tell you!" She waved her hands in the air as if she could stop the discussion. "I do not need to retire. Now, if you'll excuse me, gentlemen, I'll let Miss Brandt take over." She stalked toward the main room.

"But, Lucille—" Bruce stalked after her. "We are not through discussing this."

Without a word, Miss Penwell rounded the corner, and a few seconds later a door slammed behind her.

Bruce strode into the main room. "Now, Lucille, just a minute. Open this door." His voice faded.

Vern shook his head. "We'll never get rid of her." He walked to the main entrance. "Someone will have to kill her before she stops working at this library." He exited.

Callie turned her beautiful eyes up to Lane. "Thanks for defending me, but you didn't need to apologize. I made the decision to go with you."

"And I'm glad you did, no matter what Miss Penwell says."

She sighed. "Poor Cheyenne. I'm going to have to call her."

Lane reached into his shirt pocket. "Here are your glasses. Sorry I didn't clean them."

She gave him a faint smile. "Thanks, Lane. And thanks for lunch. It was fun, even though I had to pay the piper."

He frowned. "Does Miss Penwell have the authority to fire you?"

"No. The town council hired me, and I know they won't fire me. Actually, they've been trying to get rid of Miss Penwell for a couple months. She's been so nasty lately." Callie shrugged. "I don't know what will happen now."

"Well, she's digging her own grave, if you ask me." He glanced up the stairs. "I should finish that research on Yellowstone. Can I check out five books on my card?"

Callie walked behind the desk. "You can check out as many books as you want."

❧

"Cheyenne, I'm so sorry you had to go through that." Callie spoke into the library phone. "That must have been embarrassing when Miss Penwell yelled at you."

"No problem. Besides, it was my bad. I practically pushed you two out the door." Cheyenne paused. "Are you sure it's okay to talk right now?"

"Yeah, no one's in the building except Lane, and he's upstairs in the Wyoming room."

"I bet Miss Penwell scared off all the patrons with her tantrum." Cheyenne laughed. "By the way, how did lunch go?"

Callie smiled for the first time since she entered the library. "It was wonderful." She lowered her voice. "I'll call you when I get home after work and tell you all about it, but I think he likes me."

"Oh, Callie!" Cheyenne squealed into the phone. *She* didn't have to keep her voice down. "I'm so excited! I can't wait until you give me the entire scoop. I just *know* you two were made for each other, and I'm already praying."

"Thanks." Callie took a deep breath. "I hope we do end up

together, but I want to make sure it's the Lord's will. Right now I don't have a perfect peace about it because I'm not sure if he's a Christian." She adjusted her glasses, which she had cleaned. "I think—"

Lane descended the stairs, his arms stacked with books.

"Oh, I have to go, Cheyenne. Talk to you later." She hung up the phone as Lane approached the desk.

"Seven books, Callie." He set the pile down and placed his library card on top. "We'll show that old Miss Penwell who's boss."

Several people entered the library as Callie checked out his books. She greeted them, hoping they hadn't heard about the afternoon fiasco.

Lane made a trip to his motorcycle to place the books in the saddlebags. Coming back inside, he folded his arms on the counter and leaned toward her. "Callie, I want to apologize for getting you in trouble."

She waved away his apology. "It wasn't your fault."

"Yes, it was. I shouldn't have asked you out for lunch. In fact, I'm going to make amends. Would you go out to dinner with me on Friday night?"

Her heart leaped into her throat. "I'd love to."

"Good." He grinned then reached up and pulled off her glasses.

Startled, Callie stepped back. "Lane—"

"Just wanted one more look." His smile faded as he gazed into her eyes.

She gazed back, a wistful sigh escaping her lips.

The front door opened, and a group of kids walked in.

Lane set her glasses on the desk. "Until Friday." He strode to the door, then he turned and winked at her before stepping outside.

At least she thought he winked. His face was so blurry she

could barely make out his eyes.

Friday night. Callie hugged herself. But this was only Monday, and Friday seemed to stretch into eternity. *Oh Lord, please give me peace about Lane.*

Donning her glasses, Callie reached for the phone and dialed Cheyenne's number. This was too good to keep until after work.

nine

It was a trying week for Callie.

She didn't see Lane at all, but she saw plenty of Miss Penwell. Instead of arriving each day at two o'clock as she normally did, the head librarian came in at one o'clock on Tuesday and criticized everything Callie did. Fortunately, the library was closed on Wednesday, but on Thursday, Miss Penwell arrived at noon, spewing out more criticisms until Callie left at six.

Before going to the library on Friday morning, Callie decided to fortify herself with a cup of coffee at the Trailblazer Café on Main Street. It wouldn't surprise her if Miss Penwell arrived at ten o'clock today. She probably heard that Callie had a date with Lane after work. In fact, Callie expected the whole town knew about their date by now, thanks to Tonya and her big mouth.

A lot of the locals, mainly retired men, met at the Trailblazer for breakfast every morning. Today, eight of them—old-timers she had known her entire life, including Bruce and Vern—sat at two tables in the corner. Along with swilling coffee refills, most of the men perused a copy of *The Scout*, Fort Lob's newspaper.

Vern spotted her as she walked by. "Hey, Callie! Did you see the column in today's paper by Herbert Dreyfuss?"

She stopped beside their table. "I haven't read this week's column yet."

"Another great article about Wyoming."

"Yeah." Floyd DeWitt pointed to the paper. "We've been discussing it all morning."

"Really?" Callie folded her arms. "What's it about?"

"Yellowstone National Park."

"Yellowstone?"

Vern nodded. "Would you believe, Dreyfuss says it's one of the best vacation spots in the country. And he tells you all about it." He chuckled. "That Dreyfuss is a smart one, just like I always said."

Callie bid the men good day and left to get her coffee.

Yellowstone. What a coincidence.

❧

At 6:30 that evening, Lane guided his rumbling motorcycle down the long driveway toward the Brandt farmhouse. He and Callie had agreed to leave his cycle at her house and drive her car to Lusk for dinner. Even though Lusk was a good half hour away, it was closer than any other town, and they certainly didn't want to eat in Fort Lob where everyone could watch them.

To be honest, he was tired of Fort Lob's gossip. If it weren't for Callie, he would have moved to Lusk or Pinedale by now.

Approaching the farmhouse, he noticed Jake Brandt sitting on the porch. Lane's stomach lurched. *He's going to grill me about dating his daughter.* After all, what did Mr. Brandt know about Lane Hutchins?

Except for taking Callie out to lunch on Monday, Lane hadn't been on a date in years. He'd forgotten how much parents could worry about their daughters. He parked his motorcycle beside the house and dismounted.

"Howdy, Lane!" Jake called from one of the wicker chairs. "Come on up and have a seat. Callie should be out in a few minutes."

Lane climbed the three steps to the porch. "Thanks." He took the other wicker chair and drummed his fingers on the arms. *This is it.*

"Great weather for a Friday night, ain't it?" Jake stretched his long legs in front of him and crossed them at the ankles. "I like to sit here most evenings and watch the sunset. Course, it doesn't set until eight or eight thirty this time of year, but every sunset is spectacular. God's handiwork."

Lane relaxed. Maybe Jake wouldn't grill him after all. "I hear you're a sheep rancher."

"Yep, fifth generation. My great-great-grandparents were homesteaders in the 1880s. I have a good spread here—two thousand acres and five hundred sheep."

"Wow! That's huge."

Jake seemed pleased. "Aw, that's nothing. My grandfather owned eight thousand acres with horses, sheep, and cattle. But it's hard to care for such a large ranch. My dad sold most of the land and animals, concentrating only on sheep. I still have a few horses."

Lane gazed at the rolling hills that stretched toward the horizon. "So, all this land is yours?"

"As far as your eye can see. I plan to pass the ranch on to my son Derek. He has a college degree in range management, you know, and he's helped me with some new methods."

The front door opened, and Callie stepped onto the porch.

Lane's heartbeat quickened. She was beautiful. The summery yellow print dress she wore emphasized her soft curves and made her dark curly hair look even darker. He hardly noticed her glasses.

Lane felt underdressed in his shirt and jeans. Good thing he hadn't worn his I VISITED DEVIL'S TOWER T-shirt, which he had considered doing. But he'd decided against it since he wanted to have a shirt pocket available. . . .

She closed the door behind her. "Sorry you had to wait, Lane."

"No problem." He stood, wanting to tell her how nice she

looked, but her dad's presence stopped him.

"Here's the key to my car." She handed him a set of keys, and a whiff of sweet fragrance drifted toward him. "It's around the back." She descended the porch stairs.

Jake got to his feet. "Have a good time, you two."

"Thanks." Lane smiled as he shook the older man's hand. He liked Jake.

"We will, Dad." Callie rounded the corner of the house. "And don't wait up for me," she called.

Hmm. . . Lane followed her to the car. The evening looked bright.

❧

"You move to a different state every three months?" Callie's head spun.

She sat on the passenger side of her car, secretly thrilled to see Lane behind the wheel. Since he obviously didn't own a car, she pictured this little Honda as their family car when they got married—*if* they got married.

"But, Lane, how can you move so often? I always thought military people had it rough moving every three years. But three months?" Only fugitives did that.

Fugitives? Callie glanced at his profile. What if he *was* a fugitive trying to escape the law? She knew so little about him.

"I love moving." He grinned. "I've lived in sixteen states in the past five years, and every place was in a small town. It's been an interesting adventure, and I enjoy the change of scenery." He shrugged. "If I cover all fifty states, I figure it will take me another eight or nine years, at least."

Callie's buoyant spirit sank. *I hate moving.* "Is there a method to your madness?"

Lane's expression turned serious. "It's research, actually. By the time that fiftieth state is covered, I plan to write a book about my experiences. I'm going to call it *Living in Small-Town*

America." He glanced at her. "How does that title grab you?"

"Sounds interesting. . . ." *He sure has big dreams.* "But I've heard it's really hard to get published. Of course, you have to write the book first, and that's a lot of work."

"Oh? Do you have personal experience?"

"Well. . ." She thought about that half-finished novel in the notebook on her closet shelf, languishing next to the manuscript she had started five years ago about Fort Lob's history. "Nothing to speak of."

They entered the town of Lusk, and Callie pointed ahead. "Turn left at that stop sign. I love the Italian restaurant on West Second Street." She was glad to change the subject and decided she would enjoy this evening with Lane, whether she married him or not. "It's called Mama's Kitchen, and it has great Italian food."

❧

"You know what? This restaurant has great Italian food." Lane took another bite. He had never tasted such good lasagna in his life.

A mural of Italy's wine country covered the wall beside their two-person table, and a tiny lamp, set on the edge, shed a circle of yellow light on the white linen tablecloth.

"I guess 'Mama' is a good cook." Callie adjusted her glasses. "They always give their customers such big portions. I have enough Eggplant Parmigiana on my plate for three people, and we *have* to save room for dessert. Mama's Kitchen has the most delicious desserts."

"Ice cream cones?"

A blush spread over her face. "Much better than that, but please don't throw a spoonful of tiramisu at my left lens."

He grinned. "If you recall, I don't use that ploy anymore." He reached across the table and snatched off her glasses.

"Lane!" She covered her face with both hands and peeked

at him through her fingers.

He dropped her glasses in his shirt pocket. "Much better." He gazed into her eyes, startled again by how pretty she was. *I have to get her that laser eye surgery.*

She sighed as she dropped her hands back to the table, and he could tell she was trying not to smile. "What am I going to do with you?"

Kiss me? "Uh, I don't know. . .I'll think of something."

❧

Callie felt completely lost without her glasses. Everything was a blur, even her food.

She swallowed a bite of her eggplant. "Could I ask you a personal question?" She glanced up and blinked a couple times, unsuccessfully trying to bring his face into focus.

He gazed a moment at her eyes. "Anything."

Callie hesitated. *The power of a woman's eyelashes*—one of her sister's pet phrases. No wonder Tonya batted her eyes at every new guy she met. "Um, first of all, could I have my glasses back? I really can't see anything."

"Oh." He dipped into his pocket and pulled them out. "Sorry to tease you. Guess I'm just an insensitive cad."

She smiled as she took her glasses. "No, you're not." Noticing a smudge, she wiped the lenses with the hem of her dress.

Lane leaned forward. "So, what's the personal question?"

"I was wondering about your job. What do you do for a living?" There, she asked him. His job status had bothered her since she'd met him. "When you first came to the library, Miss Penwell asked what you did, and you told her you were an insurance salesman."

He frowned. "I did?"

"That's what she told me." Callie put her glasses back on, thankful Lane was in focus once again.

He pushed a bite of lasagna around on his plate. "Oh,

I remember now. I told her I was an *agent.*" He laid his fork down. "But an agent can be anything—a manager, an investment broker, a real estate person, an insurance man, a book agent, a spy. . . ." He tapped his chin thoughtfully. "I'll let you guess which one I am."

"You're definitely a spy."

He threw back his head and laughed so loud that other diners turned to look at him. "Right you are, Callie."

"Oh sure." She couldn't help but smile. "But really, Lane, tell me about yourself. You know so much about me. I've told you about my family, my church, my job, and even my dreams, but I hardly know anything about you." She touched his hand, which was resting on the table across from her own. "Tell me all about Lane Hutchins."

He shrugged, and his smile faded to a frown. "I have no family, no friends. I'm just a drifter, Callie." He looked down, picked up her hand, and cradled it in both of his own. "When my parents died, my aunt and uncle raised me." He looked up. "I've already told you that."

She nodded. "How did the accident happen?"

"My dad owned a Cessna, a small airplane. He had a pilot's license, and he was always jetting my mom around the country. They took a lot of vacations—without me."

Callie pictured the young couple, too busy with their own lives to take care of the little boy who needed them. She squeezed his hand. "That's sad."

"It would have been, except for Aunt Betty and Uncle Herb. I stayed with them so often, they might as well have been my parents. When the plane crashed, I was actually excited I could live with them permanently." He paused. "I've often wondered what would have happened to me if my parents had lived."

"What do you mean?"

"Uncle Herb, my mother's brother, married Aunt Betty late in his life, so they were too old to have kids. But Aunt Betty was so motherly. She loved children, and whenever I was with her, I was her son."

Callie smiled, nodding for him to continue.

"The most important thing was that she was a Christian, and she led Uncle Herb to the Lord before they married. Then, when I was nine years old, Uncle Herb led me to the Lord."

Relief flooded through her. "That's wonderful!"

Lane squeezed her hand. "I still remember him sitting on my bed that night. I was scared for some reason, scared to die. He told me about Jesus, who died in my place so I could go to heaven. And I believed."

"I'm so glad, Lane." Callie bit her bottom lip, willing the tears not to come.

"Me, too." He gazed at her. "But if I had grown up with my parents, I doubt if I would be saved today." He sighed. "Not that it's made much of a difference lately."

Callie widened her eyes. "How can you say that? Being saved makes all the difference in the world. It's going from death to life."

"I know." He looked down at their hands. "I used to be on fire for God. Back in high school, I was the student leader of our youth group, and I led a prayer meeting after school. But when Aunt Betty got cancer, I started cooling off toward spiritual things."

It looked like he would say more, but he stopped.

Callie spoke softly. "How old were you when she passed away?"

"Nineteen. For thirteen years, she'd been my mom, and it really hurt when she died. Uncle Herb told me not to blame God, but God could have healed her, and He didn't." Lane paused. "I started drifting away from the Lord. At least that's what Uncle Herb told me. And then, three years later, he died. Very suddenly."

"How did he—"

"Heart attack." Lane blew out a breath. "Like I told you, I'm all alone in the world, Callie." A resentful tone crept into his voice. "You have your parents, grandparents, aunts and uncles, brothers and sisters—I have no one. And I've always asked *Why*? Why did God take every single relative I had, leaving me to navigate through life alone?"

Callie laid her other hand on top of his. "I wish I knew, Lane."

"At my uncle's funeral, someone told me that God was trying to get my attention." For a moment, he pressed his lips into a firm line. When he spoke, his voice was bitter. "Well, if that's the way God is—if He has to kill all my loved ones to get my attention, I don't want anything to do with a God like that."

She caught her breath. *How can he believe that?* At the same time, she prayed for God's guidance in saying the right thing to help him. "Lane, the Lord doesn't work that way. He has a plan and a purpose for each life. Evidently your aunt's and uncle's work on earth were finished, so He took them home. God didn't cut their lives short just to punish you or to get your attention."

"Well, maybe not." He caressed the back of her hand with his thumb.

She clamped her hands on his to stop the motion. "The Lord has a reason for everything He does, Lane. The Bible says, 'It is God which worketh in you both to will and to do of his good pleasure.' He loves you, and He wants to guide your life." She shook her head. "Whatever you do, don't become bitter against God."

"Bitter." Lane almost spat out the word. "I never thought about that before, but yeah, I guess I'm bitter at God."

The more Callie found out about Lane, the more she realized she didn't know him at all. She withdrew her hands from his and slipped them in her lap. "I'll pray for you, Lane. Only the Lord can heal your heart."

He gazed at her a moment. "You're a good woman, Callie." Sighing, he pushed his plate away. "I know I have a bad attitude. Sometimes I have such a longing to get over it and get right with God."

"Then get it right." She leaned forward. "The Lord is waiting for you to come back to Him. He'll welcome you with open arms."

"Like the prodigal son?"

She nodded. "Yes, just like that."

He stared at his plate a moment before he looked up at her. Finally he smiled. "How about if we order some of that tiramisu?"

❧

As Lane drove Callie home, he couldn't get rid of the heavy feeling in the pit of his stomach. She had managed to churn up the bitter feelings he had buried in the deepest part of his heart. He ground his teeth together. *This is not the time to think about my problems.*

He glanced at Callie. She sat on the passenger side, looking out at the rolling hills of Wyoming as they drove north on Highway 270. She'd been quiet on the way home, and he wanted to draw her out again. He loved to hear her talk. Somehow her smooth voice made him forget about the emptiness in his heart. And tonight, when he dropped her off at her front door. . .

In the west, the sun lit the expansive sky in a spectacular array of reds and oranges, and the subject of the next article he wanted to write popped into his mind. "Give me your opinion, Callie."

She turned toward him. "My opinion on what?"

He frowned, trying to strike a thoughtful pose. "What do you think about overpopulation in the world?"

"Overpopulation?" She squinted at him like she thought he was crazy. "Where did that thought come from?"

"I was looking out at all this barren land, these hills covered with nothing but sagebrush and scraggly grass. It got me thinking how some folks are screaming about overpopulation. They say the world is too crowded."

She laughed. "You don't have to worry about that here. You could fit an entire third world country in the state of Wyoming and still have room to spare."

"Hey, that's good." He grinned at her. "I'll remember that. You know, I like these western states. They're huge compared to the ones out East."

"Wyoming is the ninth-largest state in the Union, and it has the fewest people per square mile, except for Alaska."

"Why, thank you for that tidbit of information, Miss Librarian. Maybe I should pick your brain instead of doing research."

She blushed. "I'm really not a walking encyclopedia."

"Close enough." He drove past the sign that read WELCOME TO FORT LOB; POPULATION 576. "Are there really more than five hundred people in Fort Lob?"

Callie shook her head. "Not anymore. That sign is at least twenty years old."

"Why don't they put up a new sign?"

She shrugged. "The town council never saw the need. Most of the people on the council are old, retired men who grew up here, although every once in a while a woman will get elected." She looked at him. "Miss Penwell served on the council for eight years."

"Really?" He smirked. "I can just imagine the arguments she sparked in their meetings."

"I don't know about that, but the library thrived while she was sitting on the council. The mansion was in great shape, and we had plenty of new books. In fact, Miss Penwell bought a lot of the books in the Wyoming room. She even talked the council into getting that state-of-the-art computerized circulation system."

"You worked at the library then?"

"I was in high school and worked during the summers with Cheyenne." She grinned. "We had a lot of fun."

"Cheyenne seems to be a fun person."

Callie nodded. "She's a rascal. And she's not afraid of anything."

"Not even Miss Penwell?"

"Nope. Cheyenne got us in trouble a few times while we were working at the library, and to be honest, Miss Penwell doesn't like her. Of course, Miss Penwell has very few friends, but that's the way she wants it, evidently."

"Is she dating anyone?"

Callie looked at him. "Miss Penwell? She probably hasn't had a date in fifty years."

"No, I meant Cheyenne."

Her eyes widened. "Are you interested?"

He laughed. "Would it make any difference to you?" He winked, letting her know he was teasing.

A faint blush stole across her cheeks. "Actually, Cheyenne has been absolutely in love with my brother Derek since she was a senior in high school."

"Absolutely?"

"Oh yes." She sighed. "I wish Derek would marry her, but he's never been interested in girls. He's only dated five times in his life, with five different girls, and every time it's been because one of his four sisters pushed a girl his way."

Lane threw back his head and laughed. "You'll probably have to push him to the altar."

"We've been trying! But personally, I think he has a commitment phobia. He says he's not getting married until he's forty."

Lane couldn't imagine waiting that long himself. Then again, the age of forty was only eleven years away. He might as well wait since he wanted to live in every state in the Union. On the other hand. . .he glanced at Callie. *"When you meet the right girl, you'll know."* Another piece of advice from Uncle Herb. And Callie seemed more right than any other girl he had ever met. But would she be willing to marry him and move every three months?

Continuing their pleasant small talk, Lane drove through town and turned right on Antelope Road, driving the seven miles out to the Brandt sheep ranch. At THE ROCKING B archway, he drove down the long drive toward the house and pulled to a stop beside his motorcycle. They ascended the three porch steps together.

Callie turned to him. "Thanks so much, Lane. I had a wonderful evening."

"So did I." He faced her, standing close. When the moment was right, he planned to take her into his arms and kiss her.

She placed her hand on his arm. "I hope you think about getting back into fellowship with God. Having the right relationship with the Lord is so important."

He raised his eyebrows. At the moment, thoughts about God were the furthest thing from his mind. "Uh, sure. I appreciate all your advice. Um, you know, Callie. . ." He moved closer, reached up, and touched her face—just as the front door burst open.

"Callie!" Tonya stood framed in the doorway. "You're finally home!"

Startled, Lane took a step back. Callie folded her arms, looking perturbed.

Tonya continued, a worried frown on her beautiful face. "Oh, Callie, you need to comfort Mom. Aunt Sara called, and Grandma took a fall."

Immediately Callie looked concerned. "What happened?"

"They think she broke her hip. She's in the hospital." Tonya's porcelain skin was pale. "Mom's packing to leave right now."

"Tonight? But Casper's a hundred miles away." Callie glanced at Lane before looking back at Tonya. "Well, she can't go by herself. I'll go with her."

"No, Mom doesn't want either of us to go since we both have to work tomorrow. Derek is going to drive her." Tonya glanced at Lane for the first time. "Sorry to bother you two, but they're leaving in the next few minutes." She went back in the house, closing the door behind her.

An awkward moment followed.

Lane was struck again with Callie's huge family and how they took care of each other. A seed of jealousy sprouted in his heart. "Sorry to hear about your grandmother. I hope she's okay."

Callie nodded. "I need to talk to Mom." She turned the door handle. "Would you like to come in?"

This was certainly not the way he had envisioned the end of the evening. "Uh, I think I'd better be going." He walked down the steps.

"Lane, are you sure?" Her eyes widened behind her glasses. "I just want to see Mom off, and then we can talk out here on the porch."

He shook his head. "You need to be with your family. See

you later, Callie. Thanks for a great evening." He jogged to his motorcycle.

His soul was in turmoil as he started the engine. He wished he were part of a big family like this one. Of course if he married Callie. . . He shook his head. She'd never marry him unless he got rid of his bitterness and got right with God. And he wasn't ready to do that. At least, not yet.

Making a U-turn, he glanced back at the house. Callie stood in the doorway. She waved. He waved back then fed the cycle with gas and gunned down the driveway—away from Callie and back to his empty, lonely life.

ten

When Callie drove past the front of the library on Monday morning, she noticed Bruce MacKinnon and Vern Snyder talking outside with another man. The man wore a uniform with his name embroidered on his shirt pocket, but she couldn't read it from her car. He pointed to a clipboard as he talked.

He must not be from around here.

Driving to the parking lot in the back, she spotted a white utility truck parked under the oak tree. On the side panel were painted the words WILSON AND JEFFRIES, BUILDING INSPECTIONS, DOUGLAS, WYOMING.

A building inspector!

Callie parked her car and entered the library through the back door. As she approached the checkout desk, the front door opened. Evidently, Bruce had unlocked the door for the building inspector early this morning. Now Bruce and Vern walked in, deep in conversation.

Callie placed her purse under the counter. "What's up?"

Bruce glanced at her. "Good morning, Callie."

Vern nodded. "Howdy, Callie."

They moved into the conservatory, still talking in low tones.

She followed them. "What's going on? Why was a building inspector here?"

The two men turned toward her, and Vern folded his arms. "He has just condemned the Henry Dorsey-Smythe mansion."

"Condemned!" She raised her eyebrows. "You can't be serious!"

"Vern, I'll handle this." Bruce cleared his throat. "I'm afraid it's true, Callie. This old place needs to be torn down. It's dangerous to the town's citizens."

She sighed. "I knew this day was coming, but I was hoping for a few more years. So you're going to demolish the mansion and build a new building in its place?"

"Nope, no new building." Vern smirked. "Fort Lob won't have a library anymore. This place is going flat in two months, and that will be the end of Dorsey-Smythe."

Callie's mouth dropped open.

"Vern!" Bruce gave him a stern look before he turned to Callie. "The town council has already voted not to rebuild."

"But what about our patrons?" *What about my job?*

"The townspeople can drive to the Niobrara County Library."

"But that's in Lusk."

Bruce nodded. "Our citizens drive to Lusk for a lot of things. I guess everyone can use their library, too."

Vern grinned. "You can have a big book sale, Callie. It'll be fun."

Fun? That was not the way she wanted to sell books.

❧

An hour later, Callie sat at the checkout desk, her chin in her hand, thinking depressing thoughts. Bruce and Vern had left the premises with Vern muttering something about raising all the councilmen's salaries. *He just wants the town's money for himself.*

Another depressing thought pierced her mind. Thanks to Tonya's interruption on Friday night, Lane had not kissed her after their date. And it sure looked like he wanted to.

Tonya could have waited a few minutes to tell her about Grandma. Mom and Derek hadn't left for another half hour.

But Callie wondered if she should get involved with Lane. She still didn't know what he did for a living. Sure, he said he was an agent—but what kind? Besides, she hadn't seen him since he roared off on his motorcycle Friday night. He hadn't come to the library on Saturday, and he wasn't in church on Sunday. The fact that he had skipped church really bothered her. All she could do was pray that he would get his heart right with God.

The front door opened to admit Agatha Collingsworth. "Howdy, Callie! Brought back that big-hair book."

Aggie's own hair looked bigger than ever. Today it was tinted green and teased into a swirl in the back. A green butterfly barrette resided in the fluffy nest above her right ear.

"Oh, I wish I could keep this book!" Aggie laid *Fixing Big Hair the Texas Way* on the counter. "I tried all the hairstyles I liked. Course some are a little out-of-date."

A little? Callie pulled the book toward her. "Do you want to renew it?"

"Nah, I'm done with it, but I had so much fun whipping up the styles." Agatha brushed bejeweled fingers lightly against her hair. "Actually, Lucille found me another book about hair. It's one of your own here at Dorsey-Smythe." She pointed at the reserved books. "Look behind ya, sugar. She said she'd hold it for me."

It only took Callie a few seconds to find the volume. She pulled it out. "Must be this one. *Beauty Tricks and Tips*." The model on the front cover looked like she was from the 1980s.

"Oh, look at this!" Aggie gazed at the cover. "I love it already! Wish I could buy books like this, but they just don't sell these good ones nowadays."

"If you wait a couple weeks, you could buy this one."

Aggie looked at her with an arched brow. "So it's true about this place being torn down?"

Now Callie quirked a brow. "You heard about it?"

"I heard through the grapevine about the building inspector.

And now that uppity town council says they ain't gonna build a new library."

"The inspector has already come and condemned this place."

"No!" Aggie's eyes widened. "The mansion ain't that bad off."

Callie shrugged. "I guess it is, Aggie. According to Bruce and Vern, the council wants to sell off all the books, flatten the building in two months, and have everyone patronize the county library in Lusk."

"Well, if that don't beat all!" Agatha hit her fist on the counter. "It ain't going to happen, I tell you. We'll protest."

"Aggie. . ." Callie shook her head.

"Besides, if the building was falling down around our ears, why would the inspector give us two months to vacate? I tell you, sugar, it ain't that bad."

"Maybe you're right."

"Course I'm right. This building can be fixed. How many people are in here right now?" She looked around as if expecting them to materialize. "Let's get everybody together and have a good old town protest."

Before Callie could argue with Aggie's plan, the older woman tramped into the conservatory. "Yoo-hoo, ya'll come upstairs to the conference room. We have a problem to settle." She strode to the main room and hollered the same words.

Callie rolled her eyes. Agatha Collingsworth was one of a kind, but a little hope seeped back into Callie's soul. Maybe they could save the Dorsey-Smythe library from extinction.

❧

"I can't believe it!"

"They can't tear down this library!"

"Why, this library has been here since I was a kid!"

Callie jumped up on a step stool, which was used to get to

the higher shelves, and motioned with her hands. "Everyone, calm down!"

The talk died as Callie glanced around the conference room. If only Aggie hadn't blurted out the news about the library's demise, Callie could have explained everything in a calm way. The crowd looked at her expectantly.

The library patrons ranged from a few moms with children to several teenagers and a number of older people. She estimated at least twenty-five people filled the room. Most stood clustered in groups, although several sat at the tables.

"Okay." She expelled a breath. "All we know is that a building inspector was here this morning. He condemned the mansion, and Bruce MacKinnon said the council has already voted not to build a new building. We'll sell off all the books before they tear down this place."

"How long before they tear it down?" Horace Frankenberg asked.

"Two months."

A murmur went through the crowd.

"But, Callie." Mrs. Anderson, seated at one of the tables, raised her thin hand. "What are we going to do without a library in Fort Lob?" Her head of snow-white hair quivered slightly as her blue eyes gazed up.

"I'm afraid we'll have to drive to Lusk and—"

"What goes on here?" Vern Snyder stepped into the room.

Agatha placed her hands on her ample hips. "This is a protest meeting, Vern! You town-council people think ya'll are so high and mighty! Well, we are protesting your decision to close down our library."

"You think so, do you?" Vern glanced around. "Huh! Don't look like much of a protest to me."

Callie sighed. "We're just giving out information right now. Some of the—"

"No! We're protesting!" Agatha looked around. "Who wants this library to close down?"

She waited a split second, but no one moved. "See? Everybody's in favor of keeping the library open, just as is."

"But, Aggie, the building has been condemned." Vern folded his arms. "The inspector said the floors are bad, the electricity should be replaced, the plumbing is old. The whole place is a disaster waiting to happen. Someone could get hurt."

"So the town needs to spend some money on repairs." Aggie touched the barrette in her hair. "What's a little money? We could all throw in a few bucks, don't ya'll think?"

The crowd glanced around before a murmur of voices broke out and got louder.

Callie raised her hands. "Listen, everyone!" She waited for the crowd to quiet. "We need to know what the general consensus is about this. How many want to keep the library open at Fort Lob?"

Everyone began talking at once, and several people raised their hands.

Vern pulled out a chair and hopped up on it. "Folks! You can't vote on this." He glared at Callie. "What do you think you're doing? The town council has already decided to shut down the library and not build another one."

Once more Mrs. Anderson raised her hand. "But what will we do without a library in town?" She glanced around before continuing in a small, quivery voice. "I come here every Monday and Friday—Callie knows. It takes me eight minutes to walk from my house. But I don't own a car, so how can I drive to Lusk every week?"

"Am I hearing you right, Shirley?" Vern stuck his finger in his ear and twirled it around. "You want the council to keep this library open just to support your book habit?"

"Vern!" Aggie glared at him. "That ain't nice."

"The town council is supposed to represent the citizens!" said one of the men.

"Where will the children go in the summer?" asked a mother.

Aggie folded her arms. "See? Ya'll can't close it down."

For the third time, Callie raised her hands as a babble of voices broke out. "Let's work something out, folks! Who would like to meet with the town council to discuss this?"

Hands shot up all over the room.

"Aha!" Aggie had both hands in the air. "Looky here, Vern, we are in protest mode. How about we meet tomorrow night at the Elks lodge on Pronghorn Avenue? Everyone in favor say 'Aye.'"

The ayes resounded throughout the room.

"Now, Aggie." Vern stepped down from the chair. "You're not following *Robert's Rules of Order*."

Agatha ignored him. "Tomorrow night, citizens! Seven o'clock at the Elks lodge. Ya'll spread the word. Let's go!"

The library patrons filed out amid a low hum of conversation.

Aggie thumped her finger against Vern's chest. "You, Mr. Vern Snyder, can tell the town council about the protest meeting. And if they don't show, our protest just might turn into a town riot." She cackled a laugh as she waltzed from the room.

Callie stepped off the stool. She and Vern were the only ones left.

"Really now, Callie. You can't seriously think you can change the council's mind."

"I guess we'll find out tomorrow night, won't we?"

Vern shook his head. "Bruce is not going to like this."

Callie smiled. For once she was glad Bruce was not here to intervene.

eleven

On Tuesday night, Callie stood beside Cheyenne at the back of the Elks lodge meeting room. The open windows and two fans circling above did little to move the stifling air. Both young and old citizens of Fort Lob filled row after row of folding chairs set on the dusty wooden floor. It looked like the entire town had turned out. Not one chair remained empty, and about fifty people stood in the aisles.

Murray Twichell strutted back and forth at the front of the room before taking a position near the platform with his arms folded. He surveyed the crowd.

Chance Bixby sat halfway back on the south side of the building, and Agatha Collingsworth's green-tinted hair could be seen above the crowd on the north side. Miss Penwell was missing since she had elected to keep the library open during the meeting.

Lane Hutchins was not there, either. Callie had called him that afternoon, but he seemed reluctant to come.

Callie sighed as Ralph Little, the balding treasurer of the town council, droned on about the need to close the library. A few heads in the crowd nodded when he spoke of the low taxes the citizens paid.

"Now, unless you want us to raise those taxes—" He stepped back as the microphone emitted a high-pitched whine. "We need to shut down the Dorsey-Smythe permanently."

He took his seat amid a spattering of applause. Most of the hand clapping came from the front row, where the nine members of the town council sat. Some of the other citizens looked like they had been lulled into a stupor.

Bruce MacKinnon ascended the wooden platform and took the mic off its stand. "For the past hour and a half, your town council has spoken. It is clear why we need to close the library. If there are no questions or comments, we will close this meeting." He glanced around. "Is there anyone from the floor who wishes to speak?"

Finally! Callie strode down the middle aisle, waving her hand, hoping Bruce wouldn't change his mind and close the meeting anyway. Frowning, he handed her the microphone.

Callie took a deep breath. "Citizens of Fort Lob." She paused as the back door opened and Lane slipped in. *Oh, thank You, Lord!* For the space of a heartbeat, their eyes met, and she smiled.

People began to turn around, craning their necks to see what she was staring at.

Callie cleared her throat and turned her attention to the men seated in the front row. "The town council is unanimous about shutting down the Henry Dorsey-Smythe Library. However, many of our citizens, including me, do not want to close it." She looked out over the crowd. "Now, I ask you folks—isn't the town council supposed to vote according to the wants and needs of the people they represent?"

Fortunately, the citizenry came to life, and several people shouted out affirmations.

"Let me tell you something." Callie spoke softly into the mic, and the room quieted. "Four months ago, the town council cut the library's spending to zero. We couldn't buy any new books. That's why we have to order them from Casper on the interlibrary loan system."

Several men in the front row folded their arms.

"Not only that but the council let the library's repair fund run completely dry."

"That's right!" Chance shouted. "I didn't have money to fix nothing. No wonder the building is condemned."

A murmur ran through the crowd as Bruce stood. "Callie has the floor right now, Mr. Bixby. Please wait your turn." He sat down and nodded for her to continue.

"Here's my point." She took a deep breath. "I believe the council decided several months ago to close down the library, and—"

Vern jumped up. "Now just a doggone minute!" His face tinged red as he glanced at Bruce and then sat down. "I'll refute that when you're finished."

Callie rushed on. "They have also wanted Miss Penwell to retire, but she has refused to step down from her position as head librarian."

The councilmen exchanged wary glances.

Callie caught Lane's eye. He grinned and raised his thumb in the air. She continued, more confident. "So, I believe the council's decision to tear down our library and not build a new one stems from two reasons. First, they claim this will save the town money, but they really want to raise their own salaries."

A buzz of conversation went through the lodge. Callie glanced at Vern, who folded his arms and glared at her.

"Second, they'll be able to get rid of Miss Penwell."

"Just fire her!" someone shouted. "We want our library!"

A chorus of voices broke out with similar sentiments, and several people stood to shout out their convictions. Callie replaced the mic and stepped off the platform.

Murray strode to the platform and grabbed the mic stand. "We will not have this meeting erupt into a riot! All of you—sit down!" The microphone responded with a loud high-pitched whine.

Amid the noise, Callie made her way to the back, where

Lane stood beside Cheyenne.

He smiled and placed his arm around Callie's shoulders, giving her a quick friendly squeeze. "Great job, Callie."

She expelled a happy sigh. "Thanks."

Cheyenne gave her a high five. "What a speech, girl. I can't believe how calm you were. You really told them like it is."

Callie shrugged. "I hope it did some good."

The three of them stood in the back as one townsperson after another came forward to add their support for the library. After each speech, one of the councilmen took the mic and refuted what had just been said.

After a particularly scathing rebuke from Vern Snyder, Callie gave a frustrated sigh. "The council won't budge," she whispered to Lane. "They have their minds made up, and it doesn't matter what the people want."

He folded his arms. "That's the danger of power. Sometimes it goes to people's heads."

Cheyenne tapped Lane on the shoulder. "You should give a speech."

"Me?" He looked startled.

Callie smiled. "That's a great idea."

He shook his head. "I'm not good at that kind of thing."

"But, Lane. . ." Callie placed her hand on his arm. "You told me this was one of the best libraries in the country. Most of our people have never been to another library. We need your input."

"I don't like speaking in public, Callie." He kept his voice low. "Besides, I don't think it would do any good."

"I think it would." She moved a little closer and stared up at him. "Won't you do it for your new hometown? Or maybe, for me?" She whispered the last two words and realized she was acting just like Tonya. But she stood still, waiting for his response.

Lane returned her stare then reached over and slid her glasses down her nose. His face went out of focus, but Callie stared at his eyes and blinked a few times.

He leaned down to whisper in her ear, "Okay, Callie, I'll do it for you." He straightened and winked.

A little thrill ran through her.

The microphone whined again. "Is there anyone else?" Bruce scanned the crowd.

Most of the people looked worn down. Several children had fallen asleep in their mothers' arms. Many older citizens fanned themselves with pieces of paper.

Callie gave Lane a little push, and he took off toward the front of the room. She adjusted her glasses so she could watch him.

The crowd stirred as he walked forward. Bruce handed him the mic and sat down.

Lane took a deep breath. "Uh, I'm new in town. The name is Lane Hutchins."

He paused, seemingly surveying the crowd, but Callie thought he looked nervous—like he was about to bolt off the stage. She gave him a thumbs-up, just as he had for her.

Clearing his throat, he nodded. "I've lived in a number of states during the past few years, all in small towns. Every one of those towns had its own library, but none of them were as good as the Dorsey-Smythe."

A murmur ran through the crowd.

"When I first visited the library here at Fort Lob, I couldn't believe the excellent reference section. Here was a library that had books about Wyoming in its own room. And I heard that Miss Penwell, who was on the town council for eight years—" He nodded to the men in the front row. "Evidently Miss Penwell was instrumental in buying the books in that room." He smiled, seeming to relax a bit. "The history of

Wyoming is fascinating, and you have a great collection at your fingertips. It's a wealth of information. Don't let it go! We need to fight to keep the Dorsey-Smythe Library open."

The crowd broke out in applause. Lane replaced the mic and stepped off the platform. The applause accompanied him all the way to the back of the room, with a few whistles and shouts of "Bravo!" thrown in.

Bruce took the microphone. "It is now ten o'clock, and we will dismiss the meeting. Be assured that the town council will convene to discuss this, um, problem."

Conversation filled the room as the crowd rose and began flowing toward the exits.

Callie shared a smile with Lane. "I'm glad you spoke, Lane. You did a great job."

"Thanks." He gazed at her.

Agatha Collingsworth strode toward Callie. "Oh, Callie, sugar! I must speak to ya'll. Got a minute?" Not waiting for an answer, Aggie pulled her to a corner of the room, away from Lane and the milling crowd. "I don't like the way this meeting went tonight. Do you?" Her dark eyes, usually dancing with fun, were serious for once.

Callie shrugged. "It's hard to say how it affected the council."

"Hard to say?" Aggie lightly smoothed back her hair. "Those stubborn men are going to do *nothing* about keeping our library open. But I got an idea." She glanced around and lowered her voice. "We need a petition, ya know? If we get enough townspeople to sign a petition to keep the library open, the town council will have to honor it."

"But what are the laws about presenting a petition?"

Aggie cackled. "I'm one step ahead of ya, girl! I talked to Bertram Lilly this morning over at the county courthouse, and he told me exactly how to get that council to sit up and take notice." She pulled a piece of paper from her purse. "I already made a mock-up to collect names and addresses. Look it over and see what ya'll think."

After some discussion, they agreed on a plan. Finally Aggie left the Elks lodge, which was empty now except for five people clustered near the platform, deep in conversation. Cheyenne sat by herself in the second row from the back of the room.

Callie realized she'd been standing for more than three hours. She sank into a chair in the row behind Cheyenne. "Where's Lane?"

Cheyenne swiveled around. "He didn't stay long."

"He left?" Callie sighed, tired from the emotional roller-coaster ride she'd taken in the past few days. "I don't know what to do about him, Cheyenne."

"What do you mean?"

"I really like him, but I don't think we're meant for each other."

"Don't say that. He likes you. Why, just look at the way he acted toward you tonight—staring in your eyes and whispering in your ear. I bet he'll be at the library tomorrow morning when you open."

"The library's closed on Wednesdays."

"Oh, that's right."

Callie removed her glasses and rubbed her eyes. "He's so reclusive, and I still don't know what kind of agent he is. Sometimes I wonder if it's God's will for us to get together."

"Oh, Callie." Cheyenne placed her hand on Callie's arm. "I have a strong feeling about you and Lane."

"I don't. I don't have any peace at all. He hasn't called or tried to see me." Callie shrugged. "Maybe I should just forget him."

Cheyenne's blue eyes widened. "Don't do that! I thought you wanted to marry him."

"Well, yeah. . ." Lane's handsome face popped into Callie's

mind, and she thought how easy he was to talk to. "But he's so bitter toward God. And besides that, something is going on in his life that he doesn't want me to know about."

Cheyenne shrugged. "If that's the case, God knows what it is. Personally, I think the Lord brought him to Fort Lob just for you." The dimples in her cheeks deepened with her smile. "You have to trust the Lord, not worry about the future. Take your burden to the Lord and leave it there."

"You're right." Callie sighed. "I'll pray and let the Lord take care of it." She put her arms around her friend and hugged her, which was difficult with a chair between them. "Thanks for your advice. I don't know what I'd do without you."

"You keep owing me more and more, but I know how the debt can be paid."

Callie raised her eyebrows. "How?"

Cheyenne grinned. "Make me a bridesmaid in your wedding."

twelve

"I'm checking this book out, Callie." Vern Snyder laid a slim volume on the checkout desk and slapped his library card on top of it.

It was eleven o'clock on Friday morning, and Callie hadn't seen Lane since Tuesday night at the meeting. But she'd seen plenty of Vern.

She picked up his card. "Seems like you're spending a lot of time at the library, even though you want the building to be demolished." She glanced at the title of his book—*How to Become a Millionaire in Twelve Weeks*.

"Yeah, well, you know." Vern shrugged. "It's a place to hang out. Once the library closes, I aim to spend my time at the Trailblazer Café."

She ran the book under the scanner. "Has the town council met to discuss the protests about tearing down the library?"

"Nah, we don't need to do that. This building will be gone in two months."

"Aggie Collingsworth still thinks we can keep the library open. She's circulating a petition for a revote."

"A petition?" Vern's bushy eyebrows met between his eyes. "That woman don't know when to stop. How does she know what's good for this town? Well, she don't. That's why we have a town council." He picked up the book. "This library has got to go, Callie. It's for the good of Fort Lob. Remember that."

Callie sighed as he left. Why were they bothering to petition?

The door opened to admit Cheyenne, dressed in her US Postal uniform, a mailbag slung over her shoulder. "Here's the mail for the library." She placed a letter, several magazines, and a newspaper on the checkout desk.

Callie smiled. "You're delivering the mail today, Cheyenne?"

"Yeah, Bernie's sick. But I like doing delivery. Gets me out of the building. It gets so hot in there without air-conditioning." She tapped the newspaper. "You should read today's article by Herbert Dreyfuss."

Callie picked up *The Scout*. "What's the subject?"

"The danger of power in city halls." Cheyenne smirked. "It was awfully quiet over at the Trailblazer Café—you know all those men who meet there for breakfast every morning? Most of them are on the council, and I don't think they appreciated Mr. Dreyfuss's opinion."

Callie found the column on page eight beside the familiar picture of Dreyfuss—a handsome man in his sixties with graying temples. She spread the paper on the desk. The article was called "City Hall and the Dangers of a Political Machine." Silently she read the first few sentences. "But Cheyenne, this is about New York City and the history of Tammany Hall."

Cheyenne leaned over and pointed to a paragraph near the bottom of the page. "Read this—out loud."

Callie focused on the words. " 'The political machine that wields power doesn't have to be in a big city. Sometimes small towns have a group with great influence over their citizens. A town council often runs the town, making decisions without any input from the populace. In effect, it's the old problem of taxation without representation.' " She looked up. "Wow, he put his finger on Fort Lob's problem."

"Isn't that an amazing coincidence?" Cheyenne hefted her mailbag over her shoulder. "You'd think old Herbert knew what had happened Tuesday night." She turned to the door. "Gotta run. Later, girlfriend."

"Bye." Callie perched on the stool behind her and read the entire article. Except for that one paragraph, the article didn't have a remote resemblance to Fort Lob, but the mention of the town council was certainly a strong coincidence.

Just like the Yellowstone article.

Turning to the computer, she pressed a few keys. Lane's name popped up with a list of books he had recently checked out.

Callie's jaw dropped. "I can't believe this," she muttered.

Two children brought their books to the desk, interrupting her. She checked them out then helped a young mother find some books on child rearing. Ten minutes later, she got back to Lane's name on the computer, hoping no one else would need her.

She remembered calling Lane on Tuesday afternoon about the protest meeting. She called around four o'clock, but then he was late to the meeting, not arriving until eight thirty. According to the computer, he had checked out two books at 7:15. She stared at the titles.

William Tweed: Boss of Tammany Hall.

New York City and the Political Machine.

She took a deep breath. Lane definitely had something to do with Herbert Dreyfuss. But what?

The door opened, and Aggie swept into the library. She held a clipboard in her bejeweled hand. "Oh, sugar! You wouldn't believe all the signatures I'm collecting."

Callie sighed. "Do you think it will do any good? Vern seems to think the library is history."

"Of course Vern would think that! He doesn't come up for reelection for another three years. But we'll show him!" Her husky voice sounded confident. "I just got back from Bruce MacKinnon's ranch. We had a good talk."

Callie raised her eyebrows. "Did Bruce sign it?"

Aggie sobered. "Well, no. But he did agree to a meeting with the citizens. After all, his reelection is coming up in November. He has to consider the popular vote." She brushed her fingers against her hair. Today it was back to pink and looked like spun cotton candy. "I'm so excited! We have a date."

"You and Bruce?"

"No, no!" Aggie cackled out a laugh. "As if he would want to date an old hen like me." Her smile faded. "A date for the meeting, girl, held at the Elks lodge on Saturday, August 30, seven o'clock." She tapped a red-manicured fingernail on the desk. "Write it down, sugar. We'll beat the pants off those old councilmen!"

"Really, Aggie." Callie tried to hide her smile but didn't quite succeed. "So we need all those signatures by the thirtieth?"

"Oh, I'll have them long before then. Why, that's two weeks away. Plenty of time." She placed the clipboard in front of Callie. "And I need to get your John Hancock, Miss Callie Brandt. Sign right here." She pointed to the next available line.

After Callie wrote her name and address, Aggie picked up the clipboard. "By the way, sugar, did you see that article by Herb Dreyfuss this morning?"

"Yep. Looks like we have a political machine right here in Fort Lob."

"I know!" Aggie knit her brows together. "Ya'll don't think Herbert Dreyfuss snuck into our protest meeting, do ya?"

"Well. . .I don't think so."

Aggie brayed out a laugh. "Just kidding." She glanced around. "Think I'll take a little traipse through the library and have everyone sign up." She ambled into the conservatory and soon struck up a conversation with Mrs. Anderson.

Shaking her head, Callie pulled out a reserved book. That Aggie was a real character. But. . .could she be right? Was Herbert Dreyfuss actually at the meeting Tuesday night?

Callie sank down on the stool. First the Yellowstone

article—after Lane had checked out all those books about Yellowstone. Then the one about New York, Tammany Hall, and the political machine—after he had checked out books on those subjects. And he *did* have an uncle Herb.

But that must be a true coincidence. His uncle had been dead for seven years. However, a rumor had circulated a few years ago that Herbert Dreyfuss was dead. Everyone thought it was speculation, and Callie herself had never believed it.

Maybe Lane was Herbert Dreyfuss's agent. Yes—a *book* agent. That must be the type of agent he was. And perhaps. . . perhaps Lane did the man's research for him.

"That's it!" She jumped up from the stool just as two teen girls walked by the desk. She smiled at them sheepishly before looking again at the reserved books.

Probably Lane looked through dozens of books for each article, found good material, then called Dreyfuss and talked it over with him. Maybe he e-mailed him through the Wi-Fi at the Trailblazer Café. She once saw Lane at a table in there with a laptop sitting in front of him.

With a smile, Callie nodded. She'd figured it out. And she felt 100 percent better knowing Lane's secret.

❧

A week later, Aggie breezed into the library. Callie stood at the checkout desk beside Miss Penwell, who had just arrived.

"We did it!" Aggie laid down the clipboard, stuffed with a sheaf of messy papers. "Girls, we have collected enough signatures. I am so excited I could scream!"

Miss Penwell pursed her lips. "Please don't do it here, Agatha. Take your screams elsewhere."

"Oh, Lucille!" Aggie cackled out a laugh. "Ya'll are a riot! I'm gonna drive out to Bruce MacKinnon's ranch and throw this petition in his lap. Why, practically the whole town signed the thing!"

Callie folded her arms on the desk. "I sure hope it saves our library."

"It won't." Miss Penwell turned to the computer. "This building will be gone before you know it."

A cloud of depression settled over Callie. Miss Penwell was right. The library was history, and so was Callie's relationship with Lane Hutchins. She had tried to call his apartment several times in the past four days, but there was no answer. Finally, in desperation, she had called Mrs. Wimple who informed her that Lane was out of town. He said he wouldn't be back until the end of the month.

She couldn't believe how much she missed him.

But Aggie had no such reason to dampen her spirits. "Now, Lucille, don't be such a wet blanket. I think this petition will do a world of good. And don't forget that Bruce agreed to a meeting on the thirtieth. That's only eight days away."

Miss Penwell glanced at Aggie before looking back at the computer. "Bruce may well be impressed with the number of signatures you've collected, Agatha, but some of the other men on the council won't be swayed. They have no use for Fort Lob's history. They would tear down every old building in this town if they could."

Aggie patted Miss Penwell's hand. "That's not true, hon. Besides, some of them are up for reelection this year, and they'll probably agree to give it time. At least they'll fix the electrical or something. I think—"

"You don't know the councilmen like I do." Miss Penwell wagged her finger at Aggie. "These old buildings are expensive to maintain, and they don't want to spend the town's money. They'd rather put it in their pockets."

"But, Lucille—"

"Do you know what kind of books Vern, Ralph, and some of those other men check out? They're all about finance and investing and making money. That's all they care about."

Aggie sighed, her good mood seeming to deflate for the first time. "I guess some of them men are greedy, Lucille, but that don't mean we can't persuade them to see our side." She tapped the papers on the clipboard, her voice lifting with each word. "Look at all these signatures! Why, when the men see all these names representing people—the people of our town—who want to save our library, the idea will take wings and fly."

"It will never get off the ground." Miss Penwell pursed her lips.

Aggie ignored her. "Callie, hon, why don't you go with me to see Bruce? He likes you, and maybe you can add your two cents. Ya'll can represent the younger crowd." She turned to Miss Penwell. "That okay, Lucille? You won't need Callie for a few minutes, will ya, sugar?"

Callie looked at Miss Penwell, knowing *that* petition would never fly.

The older librarian adjusted her wire rims. "Well—"

"Oh, you're such a sweetie!" Aggie leaned over and gave Miss Penwell a quick hug. "We'll be back as soon as we can."

❧

Callie hung on for dear life as Aggie's open Jeep bounced over the dirt road to Bruce's ranch, which was four miles southwest of town. Even though Aggie hit every pothole in the road, she managed to talk the entire time she was driving. Callie kept her mouth tightly shut, hoping to keep the dust and bugs out. When they finally pulled up in front of Bruce's two-story farmhouse, she prayed she wouldn't look as disheveled as she felt.

Aggie parked the Jeep in front of the porch.

Callie got out, hot and covered with a thin layer of dust. She couldn't wait to get into Bruce's air-conditioned house.

"Oh, look at these roses!" With her clipboard, Aggie pointed to the red flowers growing profusely on trellises beside the porch. "How Bruce can keep his roses growing like that in August, I'll never know."

They ascended the steps to the front door. Before Aggie could knock, Bruce opened the screen door for them. "Come on in. I heard through the grapevine that you'd collected enough signatures, Aggie." His *r*'s rolled with the lilt of his voice. "Thought you might be over today."

"Now isn't this the most gossipy town ever? I only told one or two people." Aggie walked past him into the house. "Maybe three."

Callie smiled when Bruce winked at her.

Aggie took a large blue easy chair in the living room. "I brought Callie with me to represent the younger set, Bruce." She dropped her voice and nodded at Callie. "Now ya'll be sure to jump into the conversation, sugar."

Thankful for the cooler air, Callie took a seat on the comfortable blue-and-white-plaid sofa. "Well, I—"

"Oh, Bruce." Aggie glanced around. "Every time I come to your house, I'm impressed all over again! I just love the way ya'll decorate."

"Why, thank you, Aggie." Bruce handed her a glass. "Iced tea? I remember that you like plenty of sugar."

"Oh, ya'll are just the sweetest thing!" Aggie smiled up at him as she took the glass.

Callie stared at Aggie's face. *She really likes him!* Callie had never thought of old Agatha Collingsworth falling in love with someone. But this was too funny—a down-home, overweight Texas gal falling for a sophisticated and staid Scotsman. Aggie had mentioned that Bruce wouldn't want to date an old hen like her. Evidently she had no hope for a relationship with him. *Just like me with Lane.*

Callie thanked Bruce for the glass he handed her, grateful for something cold. Taking a sip, she glanced around. She had always loved his spacious home. Instead of carpet, the highly polished wood floor was partially covered with a large, braided blue rug. A nautical theme, in blue and white, dominated the room with lighthouses on the fireplace mantel and a ship's wheel attached to the white-paneled wall.

Aggie talked on about nothing while Bruce took a seat in a wooden rocking chair. After ten minutes of her blabber, he glanced at his watch. "Don't you have a petition to give me?"

"Oh, land's sake! Course I do!" She plucked the clipboard from her lap and thrust it at him. "Now don't forget about our meeting at the Elks lodge. Just one week away, Bruce."

"Yes." He glanced through the sheaf of papers. "I plan to call some of these petitioners—random calls, of course—to make sure they signed willingly." He looked at Aggie. "I'm simply satisfying my curiosity. Did all of these people sign the petition because they want to keep the library open, or did you talk them into it?"

"Well, in all my days!" Aggie sputtered the words out. "Everyone who signed that thing wants it open, and some were stubborn as a mule about it." She glared at Bruce. "Ya'll on the council do not give a hoot for the pulse of Fort Lob. Only twelve people in the whole town refused to sign, and most of them were councilmen!"

Callie glanced between the two. So much for falling in love! She cleared her throat. "Uh, Bruce, I have a question. If the council does decide to keep the library open, will they demolish the mansion and build a new building?"

"No, I believe we'll try to renovate the Dorsey-Smythe house."

"Oh good." Callie let out a relieved sigh. "I've always loved that old place. It has so much history in it, and I would hate to see it torn down."

Bruce grunted his agreement. "But some of the council members don't see eye to eye on restoring the mansion. They don't value our town's history."

"Like that Vern Snyder!" Aggie folded her arms. "He certainly has a mind of his own."

Bruce smiled. "Like a number of our citizens, Aggie. But you realize, of course, that in renovating the property, we will be forced to increase local taxes."

"So what's a few more bucks? It's like that nice young fella, Lane Hutchins, said. The Dorsey-Smythe is one of the best libraries in the country with a great collection of Wyoming books." Aggie glanced at Callie. "Remember when Lucille went on that spending spree to get all them books?" Barely waiting for a nod, she turned back to Bruce. "And did ya'll see the column by Herb Dreyfuss in this morning's paper? 'The Influence of Libraries in America.' You'd think old Herbert knew what our citizens have been going through."

Bruce nodded. "I read it. In fact, it convinced me to be more open about keeping a library right here in our town. Our children and young people need it." He looked at Callie. "And I suppose you want to keep your job."

"I certainly do!" Callie smiled, but her smile was for Herbert Dreyfuss.

thirteen

It was good to be back.

Lane rode his Harley down Main Street and turned in at The Stables parking lot. The sun was high overhead, warming the air to ninety-seven degrees. He had removed his helmet as soon as he left the interstate, and he enjoyed the warm wind hitting his sunglasses and whipping through his hair.

For the past two weeks, he'd stayed in his house in Cheyenne, writing two magazine articles and feverishly trying to beat his publisher's deadline on a new book. He knew he'd never make the deadline if he stayed in Fort Lob. The people here were too. . .friendly. Even though he should move to a bigger town, he didn't want to. The suffocating small-town feel was growing on him.

Besides, he missed one particular person in this town—a twenty-something girl who hid her beauty behind a pair of glasses. Tomorrow would mark three weeks since their date, and he needed to give her a call.

He parked the Harley but didn't bother going to his apartment. Whistling, he sauntered across the street to Wilkins Grocery.

The bell above the door jangled as he entered, and he relished the cool air. Removing his sunglasses, he dropped them in his shirt pocket.

Jim Wilkins was checking out an old lady's groceries. "Hey there, Lane!" he boomed out with a grin. "Haven't seen you around these parts for a couple weeks."

"Uh, no, I was out of town." Lane rushed on, not wanting Jim to ask questions. "But it's great to be back, and I need some groceries. Do you have any fresh fruit, like strawberries?"

"Of course we have strawberries. That will be twenty-seven dollars and forty-three cents, Mrs. Babcock. The strawberries are full price right now, but the watermelons are a steal. And a few of our apples are on sale, too. Thanks so much, Mrs. Babcock." Jim's loud voice never varied between the two conversations.

Lane moved toward the produce section. "Thanks."

Twenty minutes later, he left the store with a carton of strawberries, a quart of milk, a box of cereal, and five frozen dinners. He walked back to The Stables and climbed the stairs to his apartment, ready to eat lunch.

He was getting tired of frozen dinners.

At six o'clock that evening, as he microwaved yet another frozen entrée, he realized he had left a book in his motorcycle saddlebag. He bounded down the stairs and out into the sunshine. After retrieving the book, he walked back to the apartment building.

The blast from a car horn made him jump. He turned toward the sound.

Callie rolled down her car window as she pulled into the parking lot and stopped. "Hey, Lane! I heard you were out of town. Welcome back!"

Lane jogged over to her car. He hadn't realized how much he had missed Callie until this moment. A deep contentment settled over him just hearing her voice.

He placed his arm above her car door and peered inside. "Hi." Why should he eat that tasteless frozen dinner when he could have a hot steak with company? "Hey, if you're not doing anything right now, how about eating with me at the Cattlemen's Diner?" He pointed down the street toward the restaurant.

"Sure! Let me park the car."

He held up his book. "I'll run this up to my apartment. Meet you here in a few minutes."

❧

Callie glanced around the crowded diner, knowing every person in this place. If only she and Lane could have gone to Lusk for dinner. But she was so happy he asked her to eat with him that she'd just have to make the best of it.

They settled across from each other in a booth by the front window. It wasn't the best place for a quiet romantic dinner—in fact, it was in the middle of everything. In the booth across the aisle, a baby was crying. The old jukebox in the corner was playing "The Candy Man," competing with the sounds of clashing dinnerware and loud conversation. Two waitresses swished back and forth from table to table, taking and fulfilling orders.

Sara Stine, Ralph Little's teenage granddaughter, brought Lane's and Callie's drinks to the table, took their order, and left.

"I hate eating alone in a restaurant." Lane sipped his iced tea. "And I'm really getting tired of frozen dinners, so I'm glad you agreed to eat with me."

Feeling like a flirt, Callie peered over her glasses at him. "Are those the only reasons?"

He laughed. "I might have another reason."

He gazed at her eyes, and Callie gazed back. A feeling of peace settled over her. *Thank You, Lord.* In that moment, she knew that marrying Lane was God's will for her. She didn't know if he was still bitter at God, or if he was really Herbert Dreyfuss's agent, or how long it would take for them to get together, but she knew without a doubt that she wanted to share his life someday.

When their food arrived, Lane stared down at his plate for

a moment before looking up at her.

Callie adjusted her glasses. "Would you like me to say grace?" She realized—too late—that she had embarrassed him at Ray's.

He half smiled. "Sure, that would be fine."

Twenty-five minutes later, after the family with the crying baby had left, they had a few moments of quiet as they ate their dessert—a brownie sundae for Lane and New York cheesecake for Callie.

Vern Snyder and his wife, Blanche, settled into the booth across the aisle.

Oh great! Callie looked out the window, hoping Vern and Blanche wouldn't notice them. But of course they had good eyesight. In fact, Blanche had small dark eyes that darted around like a bird's, seeming to take in everything at once. And she was one of the worst gossips in Fort Lob. She would strain to hear every tidbit of conversation between Callie and Lane.

Callie took the last bite of cheesecake and looked up. "Ready to go, Lane?"

"Already?" He looked puzzled. "I thought it would be nice to sit here with a cup of coffee and talk for a while."

"Well. . ." That *would* be nice if Blanche Snyder wasn't sitting three feet away. "I really should get home—"

"Hey, Hutchins!" Vern turned in his booth toward Lane. "Where have you been the past few weeks?"

His voice was loud, and Callie noticed that Vern wasn't wearing his hearing aid.

Lane paused before smiling. "Oh, hi!" He reached out and shook Vern's hand. "Mr. Snyder, isn't it? Good to see you."

Now Vern looked surprised. "Uh, you, too. But you haven't been around. Was wondering what happened to you."

"I had to go out of town for a couple weeks on some business, but I'm back now." Lane grinned. "A person can't stay away from Fort Lob for long. This small-town atmosphere just gets in your blood."

"Huh!" Vern grunted, his glance bouncing to Callie before it settled back on Lane. "So, Hutchins. . ." He folded his arms. "How did your business survive while you were out of town? I hear you're an insurance agent, but you don't seem to have any customers."

Blanche nodded. "How can you sell insurance when you don't have an office in town? No one has ever seen your office or gotten a business card from you."

Lane frowned. "But I don't sell insurance. I'm not—"

"Then why did you say you did?" Blanche's voice rose. "Did you lie to our people?"

"No, certainly not." Lane held up both hands as if to fend her off. "I never said I sold insurance."

"That's what Eloise Riddell told me, and she heard it from Iva Hockett who heard it from Lucille Penwell, and you know Lucille don't talk idle."

"I told Miss Penwell I was an *agent*. That's all I said. I never mentioned one thing about insurance."

"Then what kind of agent? What was this business that took you away?" Her voice got louder with each sentence. "Fort Lob is a very small town, young man. You just can't go gallivanting around the country without telling folks why you're leaving. We want to know what you do for a living."

By this time, several people from nearby tables were listening in on the conversation.

Lane's mouth dropped open. "Well, I—"

"Wouldn't be surprising if you was some kind of crook." Vern squinted at Lane. "A man who don't hold a job in Fort Lob looks mighty suspicious. You have to get your money from somewhere. I bet you're an agent with the black market, selling stolen jewels under the table or some such thing."

"Vern!" Callie banged her fist on the table. "How can you say that? You and Blanche are smearing Lane's reputation in front of all these people with your gossip."

"Gossip!" Blanche lifted her chin. "I have never gossiped in my life."

Callie wanted to roll her eyes, but she didn't since Sara, the waitress, came by the table to fill up her water glass. The pitcher shook, and a little water spilled as Sara poured it. The teenager gave a furtive glance at the Snyders before she left.

Poor girl. "Well, Lane isn't a crook." Callie folded her arms. "And he certainly doesn't work for the black market, so—"

"Then what kind of agent are you, Hutchins?" Vern glared at Lane. "Speak up, boy! Don't make Callie defend you."

Lane raised his hands in exasperation. "I don't know why I have to defend myself. I'm a law-abiding citizen."

Vern jabbed his finger at Lane's face. "We just want to know where you come from. You gave that speech about the library, and you said you've lived in a lot of places and the Dorsey-Smythe is one of the best libraries in the country."

Lane nodded. "It is."

"Then how come you know so much about all these libraries? How come you've lived in so many places? Only men running from the law move from place to place like that."

"Mr. Snyder, I've done nothing illegal—"

"You're lying! How do we know we can trust you?"

"Vern!" Callie jumped up. "This is ridiculous. What Lane does is none of your business. You men on the town council think you can rule everyone's life. You have too much power, just like Herbert Dreyfuss said in his column. Stick with your own business and quit bothering Lane."

"Well!" Blanche turned her face away from Callie. "You certainly are high-and-mighty, Miss Brandt. I might speak with your father about this."

"That's fine with me." Callie knew she had nothing to fear there. She motioned to Lane. "Let's go."

He followed her to the cash register.

Sara had their bill ready. She fumbled with the money Lane gave her but smiled when he handed her a ten-dollar tip.

Silently Callie and Lane left the diner. In the twilight, a warm wind whispered about them as they walked down the street to her car.

Lane opened the driver-side door for her, but she didn't get in. Instead she turned to him. "Lane, I'm so sorry. I don't know what got into Vern. I've never seen him act so mean."

"It wasn't your fault."

"Well, it makes me mad that he embarrassed you in front of all those people."

Lane shrugged and opened his mouth to speak just as Jamie Spencer rumbled by in his Mustang. The car backfired twice, making Callie jump.

She grimaced. "I wish Jamie would fix that old car of his."

"He probably likes it that way." Lane glanced at her. "Speaking of old things, could you do me a favor, Callie?"

Anything. "What is it?"

"I'd like to look at those documents again—you know, the ones on the third floor of the library." He paused. "Could you let me up there for a few hours?"

She winced as she shook her head. "Not right now. Miss Penwell is working. Unfortunately someone told her you saw some of those old letters. I don't know who it was, but Miss Penwell was really upset."

He cringed as he moved a step closer to her. "Do you mean to tell me I got you in trouble again?"

"That's okay." She looked up at Lane's handsome face, wishing they could go someplace where no one knew them.

Even right here on the street, people were probably watching their every move. She sighed. "I managed to smooth things over, but Miss Penwell is very regimented. If anything different happens, she gets all bent out of shape." An idea popped into her mind. "But you know what? You wouldn't have to look at those documents on the third floor. You can look at them in one of the conference rooms."

He raised his eyebrows. "But how would I get the box?"

"I'll get it for you." She climbed into the driver's seat. "Hop in. I'll give you a lift to the library."

❧

At eight o'clock, Lane sat alone at a conference table, reading a town document from 1936. He had entered the library through the front door and walked upstairs past the circulation desk. Miss Penwell did not return his greeting. In the meantime, Callie entered through the back door, somehow procured a box of old letters for him, and left the library without Miss Penwell discovering her. Lane felt uneasy about deceiving the old librarian, but he couldn't get the documents out of his mind. When he was finished, Callie had told him to stow the box on top of a cabinet behind two displayed books. She would return it to the third floor in the morning.

Now, unable to concentrate, he sat back with a sigh. He kept thinking about the animosity in Vern Snyder's eyes. Why did that man think Lane was such a threat to Fort Lob? It couldn't be just because of the library. That didn't make sense.

Well, no matter. Lane would do his best to live for two more months in this town—for Callie's sake.

He folded the document and took out a letter. It was dated April 8, 1899, and was written by James Thomas Lob himself.

Lane gave a soft whistle. This was just the type of thing he wanted to put in Callie's museum. He was determined to get that organization going for her. It would be privately funded—by his money. And if Fort Lob—meaning the town council—didn't want to donate all that stuff on the library's third floor to Callie, Lane would offer to buy it all, no matter how much they asked.

As he began reading, the door opened. He looked up.

Miss Penwell, wearing a bright green dress with large white polka dots, stood framed in the doorway. "Please keep this door open."

"Uh, yes, ma'am." He smiled, hoping she would go away.

She didn't return his smile. Instead she took a step into the room, her glance taking in the opened box on the table and the letter in his hand. She folded her arms over her gaunt polka-dotted frame.

"Where did you get that box?"

fourteen

The next morning, Callie decided to go to work early—really early. It was only six thirty. Last night, after she had managed to sneak the box of old documents to Lane without Miss Penwell's knowledge, he asked if she had thought anymore about his museum idea. Callie had to admit that she hadn't; in fact, it was the furthest thing from her mind. But his question piqued her interest. Was that why he wanted to look at those old documents?

Before she opened the library at ten this morning, she would spend a few hours upstairs, seeing what was suitable. Even though a museum still seemed like an impossible dream, it wouldn't hurt to organize the paraphernalia up there.

As was her custom on Friday morning, she stopped by the Trailblazer Café for a cup of coffee. After last night's run-in with Vern and Blanche, she was almost afraid to be seen in public, but then her determination kicked in. Vern Snyder was not going to run her life.

However, she was still embarrassed by last evening's fiasco.

Hmm. . .another fiasco. Maybe she should tell Lane to have Herbert Dreyfuss write a new book called *The Fiascoes of Fort Lob*. She smiled to herself. It would be a runaway bestseller.

She stepped through the door of the café and glanced around. Good. Vern wasn't sitting with the other old men. Of course, this was a lot earlier than she usually arrived. Today only three men—Bruce, Ralph, and Floyd—sat at a table, eating hearty plates of bacon and eggs with a side order of toast or oatmeal.

She walked past their table toward the order window. Bruce nodded a greeting to her, and she wondered how many people in the café knew about Vern's accusations last night.

Probably all of them.

Floyd had his nose in the morning newspaper. "Did you fellows see today's article by Dreyfuss?"

"What's it about?" Bruce took a sip of coffee.

"Overpopulation."

Callie stopped at the order window.

Ralph chuckled. "We don't have that problem in Wyoming."

"That's what Dreyfuss says." Floyd folded the paper back. "Listen to this: 'Of course, there are places on this earth that have no problem with overpopulation. As one Western citizen told me, "You could fit an entire third world country in the state of Wyoming and still have room to spare."'"

I said that. Callie spun around as the men laughed and expressed their agreement. She marched to the table. "May I see that article, Floyd?"

"Sure." He was still laughing as he handed her the paper.

While the men went back to their breakfasts, Callie glanced down at the newspaper and stared at the words. *"As one Western citizen told me. . ."* She had said that to Lane, not Herbert Dreyfuss. *Why would he say "told me"*?

Callie folded the paper and handed it back. "Thanks, Floyd."

She left the Trailblazer without her coffee.

❧

Callie drove down Main Street toward the library.

Was Lane writing those articles? Could he actually be Herbert Dreyfuss?

"That's impossible," she muttered.

A scene popped into her mind—something that happened when she was in the eighth grade, twelve years ago. She was sitting at the dining room table at home, writing a report on

Abraham Lincoln. Dad sat in the living room watching TV, and one of those talk shows came on. The special guest for the show was Herbert Dreyfuss.

Callie listened to the interview for a few moments, then she left the table and cuddled up beside Dad on the sofa to watch the program with him. He had put his arm around her shoulders and pulled her close. Herbert Dreyfuss wore a suit and tie and must have been in his fifties back then. Although from Callie's fourteen-year-old perspective, he looked old. He sat in an easy chair talking to the television host, and they discussed his syndicated newspaper column. Callie remembered because she had asked Dad what *syndicated* meant.

So Herbert Dreyfuss was writing his newspaper column at least twelve years ago, and he was still writing it now. Obviously Lane would have been a teenager himself back then, so it was impossible for him to be writing under the Dreyfuss name. Unless. . .

Maybe Mr. Dreyfuss was incapacitated and Lane was ghost-writing the articles for him. Or maybe the old man was too busy writing his books to write a newspaper column, too. Or maybe Lane actually was his agent.

"It could be anything!" Callie blew out a frustrated breath as she approached the library. Lane seemed to be adept at evading questions, but she would ask what his relationship was to Dreyfuss; she hoped he gave her a straight answer.

She drove into the library's entrance and noticed a bright green lump lying at the bottom of the steps. A green lump covered with big white polka dots.

"What in the world is that?" she muttered as she pressed the brakes.

Throwing the gears into Park, she got out and ran around the car to the bottom of the stairs. She stopped with a gasp.

"Miss Penwell?"

fifteen

Callie knelt beside Miss Penwell. The older woman was lying facedown with her right arm thrown above her head. Her hand rested in the flower bed between the marigolds. Her left hand, along with her purse, was pinned beneath her stomach. Callie grasped the wrist beside the flowers and felt a faint pulse. "Oh, thank the Lord."

She laid Miss Penwell's hand down and noticed that her index finger was covered with dirt. But Callie had no time to think about that now. She had to call an ambulance.

Wishing she owned a cell phone, Callie dashed up the library steps, unlocked the front door, and raced to the phone behind the desk. A minute later, the sound of sirens came from the direction of the fire station on Rattlesnake Road.

Outside, Callie sat on the step beside Miss Penwell. She barely had time to wonder what had happened before the ambulance arrived. Callie knew the two paramedics, having gone to high school with Joe Fonsino and attending the same church as Davin Traxler. They busied themselves—one checking Miss Penwell's vital signs while the other wheeled the gurney to the front of the library.

"Oh my," a woman's voice spoke in Callie's ear.

Mrs. Wimple, the landlady at The Stables, stood beside her. Pink sponge curlers dotted the woman's gray hair, and she wore a faded blue housedress. Come to think of it, Callie had never seen Mrs. Wimple in anything but a housedress, even at church. Mrs. Wimple's face was pale. She wore no makeup, except for bright red lipstick. Callie had never seen her without that, either.

"Hi, Mrs. Wimple. I guess you heard the sirens."

Mrs. Wimple worked her red lips around into a pucker. "What happened to Lucille?"

Callie shrugged. "She must have had a heart attack or something when she was locking up last night. That's the only thing I can figure."

Joe looked up. "She was shot."

"Shot?" Callie stared at him.

By this time, the men had Miss Penwell on the gurney with a gray blanket pulled up to her chin.

"Davin called the sheriff." Joe held up an IV bag, and the plastic cord trailed down.

Another siren screamed in the distance, and a moment later, Sheriff Fred Krause pulled his patrol car into the library's entrance. The red and blue lights flashed across Miss Penwell's ashen face as he parked by the ambulance.

Sheriff Krause hauled his large body from the vehicle. "Move along, now." He glared at Callie and Mrs. Wimple—the only two people standing there. "We don't need any gawkers."

"We're not gawking, Fred." Mrs. Wimple's curlers quivered. "Callie here found poor Lucille."

The sheriff ignored them. As he strode toward the paramedics, a tan Buick pulled up and stopped beside them. Bruce, Ralph, and Floyd climbed out. They nodded to the women and then all stared at Miss Penwell.

"What happened here?" Bruce placed his hands on his hips as he frowned.

Callie hugged herself. "We're not sure, but Miss Penwell was shot."

Ralph raised his eyebrows. "Shot? In Fort Lob?"

Sheriff Krause whirled around, which was quite a feat for such a big man. "Yep. Looks like the bullet's still in there, too, but it must not have hit any vital organs."

A shiver ran through Callie. "Is she going to be okay?"

"Sure hope so." The sheriff grabbed the waistband of his pants and hiked them up. They immediately slid back a few inches. "Right now she's unconscious, but the boys will take her to the county hospital in Lusk." He seemed to be enjoying this. "Don't worry. We'll find the culprit."

Joe and Davin rolled the gurney to the ambulance.

"But will she survive?" Mrs. Wimple directed her question to Davin and Joe.

"Her vital signs are good." Davin moved out of the way while Joe slid the gurney into the back. "Fortunately, she had the good sense to stick her purse beneath her, stanching the flow of blood from the bullet." Davin waited while Joe climbed in the back before he shut the ambulance doors and strode to the driver's side. "It probably saved her life."

He drove the ambulance out to the road and then roared down Main Street toward Highway 270, sirens wailing.

Ralph grunted. "Lucille's a tough old bird. She'll make it."

Mrs. Wimple put her hand to her throat. "Ralph! The way you talk."

Even though the August sun warmed the morning air, Callie couldn't stop shivering. "I can't believe someone shot her. Poor Miss Penwell!"

"Yes, poor Lucille!" Mrs. Wimple's pale face turned a shade paler. "There hasn't been a murder in Fort Lob since the early 1900s. The very idea that someone would attempt such a thing. . ." She shook her head.

By this time, a number of other townspeople had joined them.

Sheriff Krause planted himself in front of the group and produced a notepad from somewhere behind him. "Now, before you all leave. . ." He pulled a pen from his uniform pocket. "Let me ask a few questions." With his brows drawn down, he gazed intently at the crowd, as if looking for a criminal.

Callie waved her hand. "Sheriff, when I found Miss Penwell lying at the bottom of the steps, her hand was in the flower bed, and her finger was all—"

"Yes, yes, we'll get to that. . . ." He cleared his throat as he wrote on the pad. "The boys think Lucille was shot late last night. Did anyone hear a gunshot around ten or eleven?"

A murmur went through the crowd as Ralph nodded. "Come to think of it, I heard a shot last night but thought it was Jamie's car." He looked around. "Just one loud backfire from the direction of the library."

Several people voiced their agreement. Callie stepped to the side. She had been home last night and too far from town to hear Jamie's car or anything else. Evidently, the sheriff didn't think her information was important anyway.

He wrote something on the notepad. "Did anyone see Lucille last night before that time?"

"I saw her." George Whitmore shouldered his way to the front until he stood by the sheriff. He brushed back his salt-and-pepper hair. "I was at the library last night, and I tell you, Lucille was in an awful temper."

The sheriff tapped his face with a thick finger. "Did something happen to put her in a bad mood?"

George nodded. "She had a loud disagreement with one of the patrons. Of course, that ain't too rare—especially right before closing time."

"Who was it, George?" The sheriff's pen poised over the paper.

"It was that new fella, uh, Hutchins."

Callie's lips parted. "Lane?"

George glanced at her. "He and Lucille were up in one

of the conference rooms, and I heard her yelling at him something fierce."

Uh-oh. Callie pressed her fingers against her mouth.

"And Hutchins got mad as a hornet at her. They were really having a row, I tell you."

This is terrible! Callie's heart sank to her toes. After she had left the library last night, her conscience bothered her. Why hadn't she insisted that Lane wait until the morning? Instead, she had sneaked up the library's back stairs and given Lane a box of old letters without Miss Penwell's knowledge.

"Be sure your sin will find you out."

The Bible verse flew through her mind. Now, because of her poor judgment, Lane was in trouble.

"Guess I'll pay Hutchins a little visit." Sheriff Krause turned to Mrs. Wimple. "Doesn't he live at The Stables, Adelaide?"

"Yes, but he's not there." The red lips worked around in a circle. "He left town last night. Don't know what time it was, but it was late."

"He left town?" Callie became concerned. "Did he say where he was going?"

"No, but he took all his stuff—what little he had." She pulled on a sponge curler that was falling out. "It's a furnished apartment, you know."

"So he left town." The sheriff wrote on his pad.

George nodded. "Rather incriminating evidence, I'd say."

A murmur buzzed through the crowd.

"Lane didn't do it." Callie pressed her lips in a firm line.

Ralph leaned toward her. "You must admit, Callie, no one knows where this man came from or who he really is."

George nodded. "I bet he shot Lucille last night and skipped town."

Bruce held up his hand. "Let's not jump to conclusions. He seems to be an even-tempered sort of fellow. What motive would he have to kill her?"

"Well. . ." George shrugged. "They certainly were quarreling about something."

"I think we're finished here." The sheriff waved his hand toward the crowd like he was brushing away a pesky fly. "Go home, folks. The library will be closed today and tomorrow so we can investigate the scene of the crime. And if any of you see Hutchins, call me immediately."

Callie folded her arms. *She* would not be the one to betray Lane.

❧

Driving her Honda out of the library's parking lot, Callie headed toward Antelope Road. If the library was going to be closed for two days, she might as well go home. Sheriff Krause had cordoned off the front of the building with yellow police tape. He had searched the grounds and covered every room inside, but his investigation led nowhere. Not one clue pointed to the assailant.

She gave a helpless sigh. Who would have shot Miss Penwell? Maybe one of the council members shot her because she wouldn't retire. *That's no reason.* Unless it was a cold-blooded killer.

If only she had read more murder mysteries instead of so many history and romance books. Maybe she would be more intuitive in the psychology of the human mind and she could figure out whodunit.

Unfortunately, Lane was still under suspicion, especially by Sheriff Krause, and the townspeople seemed ready to blame him. Callie wouldn't be surprised if *The Scout* had banner headlines tomorrow morning saying, LIBRARIAN SHOT BY TRANSIENT CITIZEN.

She knew Lane did not kill—or attempt to kill—Miss Penwell. But the librarian must have discovered Lane reading the town documents, and that was Callie's fault.

Lord, please forgive me, she prayed. She hoped Lane would forgive her. She couldn't blame him for leaving town.

But where did he go?

A sudden thought made her gasp, and she hit the brakes. Making a U-turn in the middle of Antelope Road, she raced back toward Fort Lob. When she arrived at the library, she pulled around to the back parking lot and let herself in the back door.

She paused inside. *Lord, am I doing something wrong again?* But the sheriff hadn't banned her from the building. After all, the crime had occurred outside, not inside, the library.

Callie ascended the stairs to the second floor and entered the reference rooms. A row of metropolitan phone books from cities and towns in Wyoming, Nebraska, South Dakota, and Colorado lined the shelf. She found the Cheyenne phone book and looked up *Hutchins.*

"There he is." *Hutchins, Lane.* She grabbed a scrap of paper from the little box beside the computer and scribbled down his address and phone number.

Callie stuck the paper in her jeans pocket. Then she went into the conference room where Lane had been last night. Nothing was on the table. She looked on top of the cabinet where she had told him to put the box last night when he finished. The two books were displayed as they had been last night, but the box was gone—Miss Penwell must have confiscated it. Behind the books lay a folded piece of paper.

She picked it up. Her name was written on the outside. With trembling fingers, she opened the note and glanced down to Lane's signature at the bottom.

Callie, thanks for helping me with my research during the past month, but I've decided to move out of Fort Lob. It's too small for my object in small-town living, and some of the people here don't trust me.

Callie knew exactly whom he meant. She kept reading.

Thanks for all you've done for me. Sorry things didn't work out for us. I'll always remember you. Lane.

"Sorry things didn't work out for us?" Callie drew in a shaky breath that was almost a sob. *No!* Things couldn't be over between them. They had barely gotten started. What about the peace she felt when they were eating together last night? She had never felt that way about Murray Twichell who declared his love for her in the sixth grade and still wanted to date her.

Callie gritted her teeth. Lane was not going to quietly disappear, never to be seen again. She was going to find him.

sixteen

Lane paced the tan Persian rug in the living room of his house in Cheyenne. "I am such a coward!"

With a moan, he plopped down on the brown sofa and dropped his head in his hands. For a few moments, he just sat there, regretting the turn of events. "How could I have done such a thing?"

He could never show his face in Fort Lob again.

After a few moments, he sat back. He had closed the drapes on the tall floor-to-ceiling windows, and the room's darkness complemented his mood. The tiled fireplace, with three framed pictures resting on the mantel, was cloaked in shadows.

With a sigh, he walked to the fireplace and picked up the photograph of Herbert Dreyfuss—the same picture, taken eight years ago, that graced Lane's syndicated column in thousands of newspapers every Friday, the same one that was on the back cover of every book Lane wrote.

He wished his uncle were here to give him advice. But even though Herbert Dreyfuss couldn't help him anymore, there was Someone who could, if only Lane would humble himself enough to ask.

Replacing the picture, he turned back to the room. Aunt Betty's old King James Bible lay on the end table where it had lain for years. Lane remembered her sitting on this sofa, reading it every morning.

Taking a seat, he lifted the old book and blew off the dust that had accumulated on its cover. The Bible fell open to a bookmark in Philippians, and Lane glanced at an underlined verse. *"For it is God which worketh in you both to will and to do of his good pleasure."*

This was the same verse Callie had mentioned. He thought back to what she said. *"The Lord has a reason for everything He does, Lane."*

So God had a reason for taking Aunt Betty and Uncle Herb, even though He knew it would make Lane bitter?

Bitter. Yep. That was Lane Hutchins to the core. Bitter at God.

"Only the Lord can heal your heart, Lane."

He thought back to his high school days—those happy, carefree days before Aunt Betty got sick. Lane had truly loved Jesus Christ and wanted to serve Him. But when things in his world started falling apart. . .

"The Lord is waiting for you to come back to Him."

He knelt by the sofa. "Okay, Lord, I'm coming back. You've got my attention, even though Callie says You don't work that way." He let out a deep sigh. "I've taken charge of my life for the past seven years, and I've failed. Please forgive me for my bitterness and for running away from You. Cleanse my heart, Lord. I surrender it to You. I need You, and I'll need Your guidance for the rest of my life."

❧

The sun was shining as Callie took to the open road early Saturday morning. She had prayed long and hard about her decision to visit Lane. Of course, he might not even be in Cheyenne, but she had to try something.

She wasn't going to let him slip out of her life.

But she didn't want to stay in Cheyenne too long. The town meeting about keeping the library open was scheduled for tonight at seven, and she couldn't miss it.

Lane would be surprised to hear what had happened to

Miss Penwell. The old librarian was still in a coma, which was another thing Callie was praying about. If only Miss Penwell would wake up, she could tell them who shot her. Then all the rumors about Lane would die.

Pushing the car's accelerator to sixty-five miles an hour, Callie drove south on the two-lane, paved road known as Highway 270. In the last ten minutes, only one car had passed her. Humming along with the air conditioner, she knew God would work everything out between her and Lane.

She felt a bump and glanced in the rearview mirror. Something small, like a piece of wood, lay near the side of the road behind her. *I must have run over that.* She didn't think too much about it until a minute later when she heard a *thwump, thwump* noise. The back right tire began to pull with each *thwump.*

"Oh no!"

Slowing down, she pulled the car to the edge of the road and stopped. A steady warm breeze lifted her hair as she got out and walked around the back to look at the tire. It was totally flat.

Callie slapped her hand to her forehead. "Great! Just great." With a sigh, she unlocked the trunk. She hadn't changed a tire since she was sixteen. Dad had taught her when she was learning to drive, but that was ten years ago. She had never changed a real flat tire and never by herself.

Now I know why people carry cell phones. Not that a cell phone would do her any good on this barren highway. Signals didn't reach out here. She would just have to change the tire herself and pray that it stayed on until she reached Cheyenne.

She got out the jack and looked at it then looked at the car. Didn't this thing come with directions? *Lord, send me help!*

Peace flooded her heart. The Lord would be her Helper. After all, He was the Great Mechanic—He knew how to change a flat tire.

She thought about the owner's manual in the glove compartment and pulled it out. Flipping through the book, she found the section on changing a flat tire. Standing beside the car, she read the instructions as a vehicle pulled up behind her. Whirling around, she breathed out a sigh of relief.

Tom Shoemacher climbed down from his tow truck. "Hey there, Callie! Got a flat, I see."

"Oh, Tom! Am I glad to see you!" She laughed, inwardly thanking the Lord for sending Fort Lob's only full-service gas station owner. "I ran over something a few miles back, and it must have punctured the tire." She pointed to the jack. "I'm not sure if I'm doing this right."

"Well, no worries." Tom smiled, wreathing his face in wrinkles. "I'll have this fixed in two shakes of a lamb's tail. Let me get my own tools from the truck."

"Thanks so much." *Thank You, Lord. You're so good to me.*

Tom came back and set his tools on the ground. He adjusted the jack under the side of the car in front of the back tire and pumped it up.

Callie watched him. "I was afraid I wouldn't see one car on this lonesome highway. You're a real answer to prayer."

"We do have a sparse population. It's like old Herbert Dreyfuss wrote yesterday about being able to fit a whole third world country in Wyoming." He laughed as he glanced at her. "Did you read it?"

She nodded. *I said it.*

"And isn't that the truth!" Taking a wrench, he twisted off the lug nuts before lifting the flat tire from the axle.

Callie sighed, thankful she didn't have to worry about those lug nuts. It probably would have taken her an hour to get them off.

"I'm on my way to Torrington to pick up my wife." Tom

took the spare tire from the trunk and rolled it to the side of the car. "She's been visiting her sister this week."

Callie smiled. "Your wife was my Sunday school teacher in fifth grade."

Tom lifted the spare up on the axle. "Lila was pert near everyone's teacher in Fort Lob who's under thirty-five. Hasn't missed a Sunday for twenty-four years." He lifted the hubcap back in place and tightened the wheel nuts. "There you go, Callie. All fixed."

"I appreciate that so much. What do I owe you, Tom?"

"Nothing." He picked up his tools. "Although I wouldn't mind one of those good Sunday dinners your mom makes."

Callie laughed. "I'll talk to Mom, and we'll have you and Lila over one of these Sundays."

After Tom pumped down the jack and put everything away, he followed her car down to the end of Highway 270, where she turned right toward the freeway. He turned left toward Lusk and Torrington. She waved her hand out the window as they parted ways.

Callie glanced at the map lying on the passenger's seat, and her stomach clenched. It would probably take an hour or more before she arrived at Lane's house, but she hadn't given a thought to what she would say when he opened the door.

Why did you run away? No, that was no good.

Come back to Fort Lob—I miss you. That sounded lovesick.

I'm stalking you, mister! Too flirty.

She sighed. "Lord, You helped me once today. Please help me again."

A verse of scripture popped into her mind. It was a verse in Hebrews about coming boldly to God's throne of grace. She finished the verse out loud. " 'That we may obtain mercy, and find grace to help in time of need.' "

The Lord would give her grace, just when she needed it.

She smiled. She had learned that verse in Lila Shoemacher's Sunday school class.

❧

Finally!

Callie slowly drove past number 736, then she turned around and pulled up in front of the two-story brick house. Her stomach growled. She had thought she would arrive way before lunch, but the morning had not gone as planned. First the flat tire, and then she drove around Cheyenne for a while, unable to find Lane's street.

Sitting in the car, she took a moment to pray and look at her surroundings. The house resided in an older neighborhood, with a maple tree towering in the small front yard and a long driveway leading back to a detached three-car garage. Two tall windows on the left and a large bay window on the right flanked the front door of the house. There was no porch except for two steps that led up to the door. Low bushes grew on either side. The place looked inviting.

Then why am I so nervous?

With a final prayer, Callie got out and trudged up the front walk, still not sure what she would say when Lane opened the door.

❧

Lane opened his refrigerator and looked at the frozen dinners stacked in the freezer. It was one o'clock, and he hadn't eaten lunch. But he had gotten his heart right with God, and he felt good. No, he felt *clean*. With a happy sigh, he pulled out the Mexican fiesta dinner.

The doorbell rang, the sound echoing through the house. Lane frowned. No one ever visited him. It must be a salesman. *I'll just ignore it.* He turned the frozen dinner over and read the directions on the back of the box.

Ding-dong!

Lane pulled the tray out of the box and opened the door of the microwave.

Ding-dong! Ding-dong! Ding-dong!

With a frustrated sigh, Lane set down the dinner and walked to the front of the house. The entryway formed an alcove between the living room on one side and the dining room on the other. He passed the flight of stairs leading upstairs before he opened the door.

Callie stood outside, a tentative smile on her face. The wind tugged at her dark curly hair. She adjusted her glasses with one hand while the other clung to the purse strap over her shoulder.

Lane's mouth dropped open. "Callie?"

"Hi, Lane." She cleared her throat. "May I come in?"

"Oh, uh, sure." Stepping back, he motioned toward the living room. His heart pounded. Why was she here? She must have heard about what happened at the library Thursday night. *That's not good.* In fact, it was downright embarrassing.

She walked past him but stopped beneath the archway into the living room. "Nice place you have. I love a formal front room."

"Aunt Betty decorated it." He strode across the Persian rug, glad he had dusted and vacuumed after his prayer time with the Lord. The light from the afternoon sun filtered into the room since he had opened the drapes, but he turned on the lamp beside the sofa—just for something to do. He motioned to a wingback chair. "Have a seat."

❧

"Thanks." Callie glanced around as she slipped down to the chair. She couldn't believe how big this room was. The smell of lemon polish hung in the air. A brown sofa faced the two wingback chairs in front of a massive fireplace. Even though it was so formal, the room felt cozy. Homey.

On the mantel rested a framed photograph of Herbert Dreyfuss. It was the same picture that was in the newspaper and on the back cover of his books. A few weeks ago, Callie would have been surprised to see his picture in Lane's house but not now.

Across from her, Lane perched on the sofa's edge. His green T-shirt stretched across solid muscles underneath. She had never seen him wearing anything but a tailored shirt with a pocket. . . .

"So, Callie." He ran his hand through his hair before he gave her a weak smile. "What brings you down to Cheyenne?"

He's more nervous than I am.

She still wasn't sure what to say, so she blurted out the first thing that came to her mind. "You're writing those newspaper articles for Herbert Dreyfuss, aren't you?" It was more a statement than a question.

He lifted his eyebrows. "Well, yes, I am." He clasped his hands in front of him then unclasped them. "I, uh. . ." Jumping up, he walked to the mantel and picked up the picture of Dreyfuss. "This was my uncle Herb."

Callie's lips parted. "But he's been dead for seven years."

He nodded.

"So. . .the rumor is true? Herbert Dreyfuss is dead?"

Lane sighed. "Unfortunately, yes."

"And you're writing everything? Even the history books?"

"Yep." He smiled, seeming relieved to admit it. He motioned for her to follow him to the opposite side of the room, stopping at a narrow bookcase that Callie had not noticed before. Rows of books, all by Herbert Dreyfuss, filled the shelves.

She paused by his side. "Wow, Lane. This is amazing."

He pulled out *A History of Gunfights in America* from a shelf that held six more books, all with the same spine. "When I donated those two books to the library, I got them right here. These are my author's copies." He grinned. "So when you said they were expensive and I said it was nothing, I meant that literally."

Callie shook her head. "I just can't believe this."

He handed the book to her. "For you."

"Oh, how sweet." She took it. "Thank you, Lane. You'll have to sign it for me."

"I'll do that."

She studied the cover with the author's name blazoned across the top. "But, Lane, why are you writing under your uncle's name and not your own?"

His smile faded. "That's a long story." He motioned toward the chairs, and she took her seat.

Lane lowered himself to the sofa, again perching on the edge. "Uncle Herb was a prolific writer, but he struggled with his writing. He never gained the fame he wanted."

Callie adjusted her glasses. "I remember seeing him interviewed on TV when I was fourteen."

"Really?" He smiled. "I was seventeen. That was his only TV interview, and it was live. Aunt Betty and I were glued to the television."

"My dad and I were the only ones who saw it at our house." Hmm. . .she had been watching Lane's *uncle* those many years ago. "So how did you start writing under your uncle's name?"

He lifted his hands then let them drop. "I used to help Uncle Herb edit his articles, especially after Aunt Betty passed away. He taught me everything he knew about writing. Just before he died, he signed a book contract—his first one." He gave her a rueful smile. "He was so excited. We sketched out the book together, and then he suddenly passed away."

"That must have been a terrible shock for you."

"It was." Lane took a deep breath. "I wrote to his editor, Mr. Porterfield, and told him my uncle died. I thought he would cancel the contract, but he asked me to write the book and send it in." He shrugged. "I thought it would honor Uncle Herb's memory if I fulfilled the contract with a book under his byline."

Lane walked to the fireplace and picked up his uncle's photo. "That book sold so well that it was on the *New York Times* bestseller list for thirty-six weeks. No one was more surprised than Mr. Porterfield."

"So you wanted to keep writing books under your uncle's name."

Lane turned to her. "No, I wanted to write them under my own name, but the editor wouldn't let me." He shook his head. "I was so naive about publishing. Mr. Porterfield talked me into signing an eight-book contract as a ghostwriter for Uncle Herb. So I did."

Callie's eyes widened. "Eight books?"

He nodded. "I just sent in the eighth one last week." He perched again on the sofa, clasping his hands between his knees. "Since the books sold so well, Mr. Porterfield has become very unscrupulous. Over and over, he's denied the fact that Herbert Dreyfuss is dead. Now most people, especially the general populace, think Herbert Dreyfuss is alive and well, and I haven't been able to do a thing about it."

Callie shook her head. "And you've kept this to yourself for seven years?"

"It's nice that I can finally tell someone." He gave her a sad smile. "I'm glad it was you."

"Oh, Lane." Callie gazed at his handsome face.

"And another thing. . ." He bowed his head, pausing, as if he was struggling for words. "I finally had a good talk with God, Callie." He looked her in the eye. "I got it right and came back, just like you told me. I have such an incredible peace in my heart I can hardly believe it."

"Praise God," Callie whispered.

Lane stood and paced behind the sofa. "I've been praying about what to do. First of all, I'm going to get a good agent who can advise me. Mr. Porterfield has been pestering me to sign another contract, but I'd like to part company with him. Then I plan to tell the world my name is not Herbert Dreyfuss, no matter what the fallout."

She nodded. "You need to publish books under your own name."

"That's been my dream for years." He stopped pacing to face her. "Hopefully a good editor will accept me."

"I think the publishing world will welcome you, Lane. After all, you're a bestselling author. You could write that book about living in small-town America under your own name."

"I'm not sure if I should keep moving to small towns in America." He started pacing again. "That was something I decided to do without considering God's will. Now I think He wants me to settle down—somewhere. I don't know what my future holds, but I want to follow His leading."

Callie's heart took an unexpected leap. She walked to where he stood. "I'm so glad to hear you talk like that. God will show you His will because He's working in your heart. You just have to trust Him."

He stepped toward her until they were only a few inches apart. "Callie, if God hadn't brought you into my life. . ." Leaving the sentence dangling, he removed her glasses and set them on the end table.

For a moment, he gazed into her eyes and Callie gazed right back. He pulled her into his arms. "You're so beautiful."

He kissed her, briefly and hesitantly, as if he weren't sure what her reaction would be. Lifting his head, he looked at her.

"Kiss me again, Lane," she whispered.

He did—several times, with his kisses becoming more passionate and ending with one slow, deep kiss.

When they finally parted, Callie rested her head against his shoulder. They stood in each other's arms for a long time.

Callie gave a contented sigh. *This is where I belong.*

seventeen

I'm falling in love with Callie Brandt!

Nothing had prepared Lane for the feelings that coursed through him when he kissed her. He wanted her in his arms forever—or at least for the rest of his life.

His stomach growled.

"Oh!" He dropped his arms. "Excuse me." How embarrassing.

Callie stood back and giggled. "You must be hungry. Me, too."

"You are? Hey, let's go out to eat."

"Okay." She gazed up at him, a smile playing on her lips. "You'll have to pick out the restaurant because I have no idea what's in Cheyenne."

Lane thought for a moment. Fast food? Or should they go to a nice sit-down restaurant with a quiet, romantic atmosphere? "I know just the one." He picked up her glasses from the end table and handed them to her.

She raised them to her face. "Thanks."

"Wait!" Lane caught her wrist.

She paused with her glasses in midair and looked up at him.

"Just wanted one more look."

"Oh, Lane." She gazed back into his eyes.

He bent over and brushed a kiss against her lips. "Ready to go?"

❧

Callie could not believe the events that had transpired or the peace in her heart. *Thank You, Lord!* He had worked everything out for good—far better than she could have asked or imagined.

Arriving at a fancy restaurant on the outskirts of Cheyenne, Callie felt underdressed in her jeans and T-shirt, even though that was what Lane was wearing. They were seated at a quiet table in the back corner, given menus, and, fifteen minutes later, ordered their food. He ordered a rib eye steak that was twice the price of any entrée at Mama's Kitchen. She ordered one of the least expensive items—baked chicken.

After the waiter left, Callie leaned across the small two-person table. "This is an expensive place, Lane."

"Being rich has its perks." He winked at her.

The realization that Lane was rich—probably a millionaire—made her sit back in silence. She had always thought of him as poor and starving. After all, he lived in a cheap apartment in Fort Lob and ate frozen dinners.

Fortunately, he saved her from commenting. "I thought you'd be working at the library today, Callie. Don't you always work on Saturday?"

"Oh!" Her eyes widened as another realization hit her. "I completely forgot!"

He frowned. "You forgot to work today?"

"No, not that." Callie folded her arms on the table and leaned forward. "The reason I drove down here was to tell you about Miss Penwell. On Thursday night, something terrible happened to her."

"Thursday night?" Lane looked wary. "What happened?"

"Someone shot her and left her for dead. Sheriff Krause has no idea who did it. But she survived, and she's in the hospital right now, in a coma."

Lane stared at her a moment before he breathed out a heavy sigh. "Oh, that's just great!" He ran his hand through his hair. "My doom is sealed. I suppose there's a warrant out for my arrest." His eyes darted around the room.

Callie's scalp prickled. "Lane? Did you—" She pushed her

chair away from the table. "*You* didn't shoot Miss Penwell, did you?"

"What?" His confused look disappeared as he focused on her. "No! No, of course not. It's just that she found me reading that stuff from the box Thursday night, and I totally lost it."

Callie bumped her chair back up to the table. "You lost the box?"

"No, I lost my temper." He pressed his lips into a firm line before he spoke. "I have never yelled at another human being like I yelled at Miss Penwell." He pounded his fist on the table. "The things I accused her of—even *I* can't believe some of the things I said." His voice softened. "I'm so ashamed."

Callie placed her hand over Lane's fist. "Everyone knows what Miss Penwell's like. I'm sure she provoked you to anger."

He gave a rough laugh. "She provoked me, all right. The whole library heard me. It was so embarrassing." He picked up her hand and cradled it in his. "I'll never be able to go back to Fort Lob now."

"Don't say that." She squeezed his fingers.

"Callie, you're the only good thing in that town. The only true friend I have." He shrugged. "Some of the townspeople are friendly—in a nosy, curious way. But I never made friends with any of them." He sighed. "And then there are those who don't like me at all."

"There are good and bad people in every town, but you have as much right to live there as anyone else. The town council is having that meeting tonight about the library." She gave his hand another squeeze. "I was hoping, especially after what happened this afternoon between us, that you'd come back with me." She cocked an eyebrow.

He looked at her thoughtfully for a moment. "Well. . ." He lifted her hand to his lips and kissed it. "I'll go with you,

Callie, but I'm not sure what's going to happen to me."

She smiled. "What could possibly happen?"

❧

Lane decided to drive his Mazda to Fort Lob. He parked Callie's Honda in the garage at his house while she stood beside his car on the street and waited for him.

After closing the garage door, he walked down the driveway. "We can come back and get your car tomorrow after church. Then I'll ride my motorcycle back to Fort Lob."

She leaned against the black Mazda. "Okay, but let's make that after church and after Sunday dinner at my parents' house. Then we'll drive down here."

He grinned as he stopped in front of her. "I'm all for Sunday dinner."

Even with her glasses on, Callie looked beautiful to him. Impulsively he took her in his arms and kissed her.

Callie breathed out a wistful sigh when they parted. "Why, Lane Hutchins, that's the first time you've kissed me with my glasses on."

He laughed. "It works." He leaned down and kissed her again lightly.

"What will the neighbors think?" Callie tried to give him a stern look.

He grinned. "They'll think that Lane has finally fallen in love."

Callie gasped. "You—you have?"

Lane gazed into her magnified eyes. "I've never felt for another woman what I feel for you, Callie. I love you."

She breathed out another sigh. "I love you, too."

After that exchange, he had to kiss her again.

❧

They finally got on the road.

The closer Lane drove to Fort Lob, the more nervous he

became. He exited the freeway at Highway 20. "Who do you think shot Miss Penwell?"

Callie shook her head. "I have no idea. Miss Penwell didn't have many friends, and she had a tendency to argue about the least little thing with anyone who crossed her." She folded her arms. "It could have been anyone."

Lane glanced at her. "Remember what Vern Snyder said to us after we ate lunch at Ray's?"

Callie knit her brows. "What?"

"He said someone would have to kill Miss Penwell before she'd quit her job."

"Oh." Callie's eyebrows shot up. "Yes, I do remember that." She looked at Lane. "And he was so mean to you. I wouldn't put it past Vern to get in an argument with Miss Penwell and shoot her. She was good at provoking people."

"How well I know," Lane muttered. *But thank God, He forgave me.*

She gasped. "I just thought of something. Vern didn't show up yesterday morning at the library when the ambulance came." She looked at Lane. "He's usually right in the middle of everything. I wonder why he wasn't there."

Lane shrugged. "Looks suspicious if you ask me."

They drove past the Fort Lob population sign and down Main Street.

"Wow, this place is deserted." Callie looked from one side of the street to the other.

All the stores had Closed signs in their windows, and not one person walked down the sidewalks. Only a few cars were parked at the edge of the street.

"It's a ghost town." Lane turned onto Pronghorn Avenue. The Elks lodge parking lot was packed with cars and trucks. "Looks like everyone in the town is here."

"I wouldn't be surprised." She glanced at her watch. "It's 7:03.

We're only a couple minutes late."

Lane pulled his Mazda into an empty space between two cars. "I don't know if I'm ready for this."

"Ready for what?" Callie touched the door handle. "It's just a meeting, even though it's very important. I'm praying the town council will keep the library open."

He was praying, too, although he had a different petition.

❧

Callie slipped her hand into Lane's as they walked through the open doorway. The building was so full they could barely step inside. Dozens of people stood at the back. She and Lane took up a spot near the back wall behind Arnold Steiner and Lester Griggs. The two men effectively blocked her view, and the room was stiflingly hot. She glanced at Lane. He was taller and didn't seem to have any problem seeing the front.

Callie took a step to the left, closer to Lane, and peered between Arnold and Lester. The chairs were filled with older men and women. Aggie's big hair—tinted purple—stuck up above the crowd. Murray Twichell, dressed in his dark green uniform, paced at the front with his arms folded.

Standing on the platform, Bruce MacKinnon spoke into a microphone. Callie stood on tiptoe so she could see him. After speaking for several minutes, he let a couple of council members speak. The men had formulated a plan for renovating the library.

Finally Bruce spoke again. "Let us sum up our meeting thus far. In November, an addendum will be added to the ballot concerning the Dorsey-Smythe Library. If you as townspeople are willing to raise your taxes, we can renovate the old building."

Ralph Little moved behind the mic. "Now if the vote passes. . ." He glanced at some notes in his hand. "With the number of citizens in Fort Lob and the amount of money needed to renovate the library, each family will have their local taxes raised about 300 percent."

"Three hundred percent!" someone shouted.

"That's an outrage!" another man said.

People jumped to their feet in protest. The noise in the room grew like a tidal wave until everyone was talking at once.

Lane frowned and leaned toward Callie, speaking in her ear. "Can you believe they're milking the townspeople like this? The council doesn't want to keep the library open, and they're hitting people in their wallet so they'll vote against refurbishing the library."

"I think you're right." Callie's spirits sank. They were going to lose the library after all.

"Quiet, everyone!" Murray stood at the microphone and waited until the noise settled down. "If you have something to say, come to the mic. We will proceed in an orderly fashion." He stepped to the side as Bruce came back.

"Thank you, Murray." Bruce surveyed the room. "Does anyone wish to voice their opinion?"

With a determined glint in his eye, Lane huffed out a breath. "Come on." He pulled Callie's hand as he excused himself between the people standing in front of them.

The crowd at the back parted. Lane and Callie reached the middle aisle between the crowded chairs, and Lane strode down to the front, pulling her along behind him. She heard a gasp from some of the women and wondered if it was because Lane had reappeared after Miss Penwell was shot. But maybe it was because she and Lane were holding hands in public.

As Lane reached the front, Murray's mouth dropped open. But he clamped it shut as he stepped forward. When he opened it again, he declared, "Lane Hutchins, you are under arrest for the shooting of Miss Lucille Penwell."

eighteen

After another gasp from the audience, the room became as silent as a cemetery.

Oh that Murray! Callie stepped forward. "Just a minute, Murray. Lane has something to say on behalf of the library."

Murray glanced between the two of them, and his eyes dropped to their entwined hands. "Okay. I'll give you five minutes, Hutchins. But there's a warrant out for your arrest, and as a duly authorized peace officer of Wyoming, I am taking you into custody so Sheriff Krause can question you. Just remember that anything you say can be used against you in a court of law."

Callie rolled her eyes.

Lane just nodded. Still holding her hand, he mounted the steps to the platform where they stood together.

He left the mic on its stand. "Uh, hello, I'm Lane Hutchins. I spoke at the last meeting about the Dorsey-Smythe Library. As I said before, it's one of the best in the country."

He glanced at Callie, and his face was pale. She smiled at him, squeezing his hand. She wasn't sure what he wanted to say, but she would support him, no matter what it was.

Lane cleared his throat. "All of you know about Herbert Dreyfuss, the famous author." He paused. "He's my uncle."

A murmur flitted through the crowd.

"What you might not know is that Herbert Dreyfuss has been dead for seven years."

This comment caused more than a murmur. Callie looked at the faces in the audience, some registering shock and others hardening into disbelief. A few people nodded their heads as if they had heard the rumor.

"It's true." Lane raised his free hand to stop the chatter. "Seven years ago, my uncle had a heart attack and died. But I had been editing his writing, so I kept his syndicated newspaper column going, and I wrote his books."

"So you're Herbert Dreyfuss?" a man shouted out.

A tiny smile graced his lips, and he nodded. "I'm the author behind his name."

"Wow." The man stood, and Callie saw that it was Glen Massey, a middle-aged rancher who lived near the Brandts. "We have a famous person in our midst, folks."

This comment caused an outbreak of more conversation. Callie saw a lot of smiles, and she smiled back, squeezing Lane's hand.

He glanced at her with his own smile, and she was glad to see his color had returned.

"As you can imagine. . ." Lane spoke into the microphone, and the crowd quieted. "Being a bestselling author brings in quite a bit of revenue."

He paused as the audience laughed.

"Therefore, in order to save all of you from having to pay higher taxes, I'd like to donate $500,000 to renovate the Dorsey-Smythe mansion."

New exclamations burst out along with a round of applause, and the audience seemed to rise as one and move toward the front. As Lane and Callie stepped off the platform, they were surrounded by townspeople. One after another pumped Lane's hand.

Callie stood back. She had never seen Lane so happy. He was finally getting the recognition he deserved.

Murray walked up to Lane's side. "All right, folks. Step back. Give us room here."

The crowd melted back at his authoritative voice.

"There is still the matter of Miss Penwell's shooting." Murray turned to Lane. "You are under arrest, Hutchins. You have the right to remain silent." He drew a pair of handcuffs from his back pocket. "Anything you say can be used against you in a court of law." Pulling Lane's arms behind him, Murray snapped the handcuffs on his wrists.

"Murray. . ." Callie couldn't believe this was happening. "Lane is innocent. He didn't shoot Miss Penwell."

"Sorry, Callie. I'm taking him over to the sheriff's office for questioning." He glanced around at the silent crowd. "No one needs to follow us." He gave a pointed look at Callie before grabbing Lane's arm and pulling him to the door.

With his head bowed, Lane walked away. He didn't look back.

Callie's shoulders drooped. She couldn't imagine what Lane was feeling at this moment. He must be so embarrassed. She stood by the platform as the crowd dispersed. Even though Bruce hadn't dismissed the meeting, people left the building, talking with each other in low tones until the hall was almost empty.

In a few minutes, the sound of sirens screamed outside. Listening, Callie breathed out a frustrated sigh. Of course Murray would have to turn on the siren. The sound faded as the car traveled down Main Street and Rattlesnake Road, all the way to the sheriff's office. She closed her eyes. *Lord, please work this out according to Your will. Give Lane peace—*

"Well, Callie." Vern Snyder strode up with his wife, Blanche, trailing behind him. "Guess Hutchins thought he could buy his way out of this one."

Callie frowned. "That's not true, Vern."

"Huh! He's just sweet-talking you, Callie. Do you really think he's Herbert Dreyfuss? He's lying through his teeth."

Callie folded her arms. "But he *is* Herbert—"

"That half million dollars will never show up. You watch."

Blanche clicked her tongue. "That man don't look rich to me."

"Everyone knows he shot Lucille." Vern smirked. "The way he was arguing with her on Thursday night, then he ups and leaves town. Of course he shot her."

"Who else would have done it?" Blanche shook her head. "We've known everyone in Fort Lob for years, but he's a total stranger."

Callie knew it wouldn't do any good to argue with them. "Lane will be proven innocent."

"Says you." Vern waggled his finger at her. "You'd better stay away from him, Callie. He's a dangerous criminal."

She gritted her teeth. "I wouldn't be surprised if you shot Miss Penwell, Vern."

"Me?" Raising his eyebrows, he pointed to his chest.

"You said someone would have to kill Miss Penwell before she stopped working at the library. Remember?"

"Huh!" Vern squinted at her. "It just so happens I have an alibi. After me and Blanche ate at the Cattlemen's Diner, we went to Blanche's brother's house near Douglas and spent the night there."

Blanche raised her chin. "We are innocent of the frightful goings-on that happened to poor Lucille."

Vern took his wife's elbow. "I hope Hutchins can cool his heels in jail for a few years."

Gritting her teeth, Callie watched them walk away. Okay, so it wasn't Vern. But it also wasn't Lane.

She followed the Snyders at a discreet distance out the door. She was going to find out who shot Miss Penwell if it took her all week.

❧

Callie knocked on the door of the small white clapboard

house on Bison Road. She had called George Whitmore who gave her a list of everyone he could remember at the library Thursday night. One by one she visited them, and one by one she crossed off their names.

It was Sunday afternoon, and that depressed Callie. She and Lane should have been on their way to Cheyenne by now to pick up her car. Instead, she was talking to townspeople, trying to figure out who shot Miss Penwell so Lane could get out of jail.

Glen Massey had given her a ride home last night, and Murray had brought Lane's car keys to their house this morning. Now she was driving Lane's Mazda around, thankful she had some wheels.

She knocked again. *Isn't he home?* She walked down the porch and looked in the living room window, cupping her hands around her face. Yep, there he was, sitting on a La-Z-Boy recliner, watching television.

He probably didn't hear the door. She knocked on the window. Startled, he looked up. She smiled and waved. He got up, and she noticed a gun cabinet on the other side of the room. *Hmm...*

Chance Bixby opened the door, wearing a white T-shirt and blue shorts.

"Hi, Chance." She smiled. "I was wondering if I could come in and talk to you for a minute."

He frowned. "What about?"

Callie paused. Chance was usually so nice to her, always relaxed and friendly. But today he looked tired, and the stubble on his face told her he hadn't shaved for a few days.

"You're not sick, are you, Chance?" Come to think of it, she hadn't seen him at the meeting last night.

"I feel fine. Now what do you want?"

Callie stepped back, surprised at his curt tone. "I'm, um,

trying to find out who shot Miss Penwell, and I heard you were at the library Thursday night."

"So you're blaming me? Is that why you're here, Callie?"

"No. . ." She smiled, softening her voice. "I was just wondering if you heard or saw anything suspicious when you were leaving the building."

He stared at her.

"The fact is. . ." She swallowed as Lane's arrest hit her anew. "Lane argued with Miss Penwell Thursday night, and then he left town. So Murray arrested him on circumstantial evidence." Tears filled her eyes. "He didn't do it, Chance! Someone else shot Miss Penwell, but Lane is being held in jail until the police figure out who's responsible."

Chance opened his mouth then closed it. He shrugged. "I can't help you. Sorry." He stepped back and shut the door in her face.

Stunned, Callie walked back to the car. Either Chance didn't want her interrupting his television program, or he was hiding something.

nineteen

I only want to see one person in this world.

But visiting Lane at the jail would have to wait.

From Chance's house, Callie drove down Bison Road to Main Street, turned right, and drove three miles to Highway 270. She would visit the county hospital in Lusk. Perhaps Miss Penwell had awoken from her coma. At least, Callie prayed so. That would certainly speed things up as far as arresting the correct assailant was concerned.

After parking the Mazda near the hospital entrance, she took the elevator to the third floor. While the elevator slowly made its way up, Callie had time to reflect. She wished Cheyenne was in town, but she and her dad were visiting relatives in North Dakota. Tonya had driven to Douglas yesterday to pick Mom up at Grandma's house. Dad and Derek were the only ones at home. They sympathized with Callie, but it wasn't the same kind of empathy a woman would give her.

The elevator jerked open at the third floor, framing Murray Twichell.

He smiled. "Hey, Callie!" The smell of his aftershave floated around him.

Frowning, she stepped out of the elevator. Murray was the *last* person she wanted to see. "Is Miss Penwell still in a coma?"

"Afraid so." He motioned down the hallway. "She's in Room 312, only two doors down."

"Thanks." Callie took a few steps toward the room before

she realized Murray was striding beside her.

"I'll warn you—she doesn't look good." Murray pushed open the door to Room 312. "She might not make it."

A single bed took up the small space. Callie walked in, and Murray followed her. Tears filled Callie's eyes as she stood at the bed rail and gazed at the woman she had worked with for ten years. Miss Penwell's cheeks had sunken in below her cheekbones, making her look even more like a skeleton. Dark circles puffed below her closed eyes.. Several tubes fed into her arms, and a monitor beeped in the corner.

Murray stood beside her. "She looks bad, doesn't she?"

Callie nodded. "I've always wondered if she was a Christian, but I never talked to her about it. I wish I had." She sighed. "Now all I can do is pray."

He put his arm around Callie's shoulders. "You could witness to her now. They say patients in comas can sometimes hear people talking."

Callie leaned over the bed and felt Murray's hand slip off her shoulder. "Miss Penwell? It's me, Callie. I'm praying for you, and I'm especially praying that you've accepted Jesus as your Savior. He loves you, Miss Penwell. He's waiting with open arms for you to come to Him as a little child. Please accept Him." She bit her lip as she stood upright and glanced at Murray. "It seems like too little too late."

Murray shrugged. "We can pray for God to work."

"Oh, I thought of something else." She leaned over Miss Penwell. "Lane apologizes for what he said to you Thursday night. He said he's so ashamed. If he were here, I'm sure he would ask your forgiveness."

Murray walked to the door and stood there with his arms folded while Callie continued.

"Lane is being held in custody in jail. The police think he shot you, Miss Penwell, but we both know that isn't true." Callie grabbed the older woman's thin hand. It was surprisingly warm. "I'm praying that you'll come out of your coma. We all want you to get better. You need to fight, Miss Penwell. Fight! With God's help, you can make it. You can be as good as new."

She looked at Miss Penwell's hand, so thin with blue veins crossing under the skin. Her fingernails looked dry, and her index finger—

"Murray, I just remembered something."

"What is it?" He strode to her side.

Callie showed him Miss Penwell's hand. "When I picked up her wrist to check her pulse, there was a lot of dirt on her index finger."

"Wasn't her hand resting in the flower bed?" He raised his eyebrows. "That's why it was dirty."

"But, Murray, I think she dug this finger in the dirt." She looked at him. "We should go to the library and see what that soil looks like."

He shrugged. "Sure, we can look, but the sheriff already combed the entire area. He didn't find a thing."

Callie laid Miss Penwell's hand down on the bed. "I'm going back."

❧

At the library, Callie ducked under the yellow police tape that crossed the front of the building. She knelt beside the marigolds. "Her hand was right here." She parted the flowers carefully.

Murray hunched down beside her. "I doubt if you'll find anything suspicious."

She looked at him. "That's the trouble with you, Murray. You've never had any imagination. You were always content to just look at the surface of things instead of digging deeper—like Miss Penwell evidently did."

His blue eyes widened, and he spread out his hands. "What have I done now?"

"I'm sorry." She breathed out a sigh. "I'm just frustrated, I guess." But it did feel good to vent. "I'd better keep my mind on our investigation." Peering beneath the marigolds, she caught her breath.

"What is it?" He leaned closer.

"It looks like two initials." Callie studied the tiny furrows in the soil. "This first one is definitely a *C*, and this one is a—"

"*D*, maybe?"

"I think it's a *B*. Yep, that's it. *C. B.* I bet Miss Penwell thought she was going to die, and she was pointing out the murderer."

Murray sat back on his haunches. "Why, Callie Brandt! Those are your initials." A stern gleam pierced his eye. "And you had a good motive to kill her, too. Once she was out of the way, you would become the head librarian by default."

"Murray! I didn't shoot her!" She couldn't believe he would even consider that.

"Okay, maybe not." He grinned. "But who else has those initials?"

Callie thought for a moment before she grabbed Murray's arm. "Chance Bixby! And I visited him this afternoon. He was acting awfully strange."

"I can't imagine Chance shooting Miss Penwell." He glanced at Callie. "But maybe I should use my imagination for once."

She laughed. "That's the idea." Then she thought of something else. "He has a gun collection. I saw it in his living room."

Murray stood. "I'll radio Sheriff Krause and see if he wants me to visit Chance."

"And I'm going to the jail to visit Lane." Standing, she dusted her hands off.

He cocked his head. "You really like him, don't you?"

She smiled, thinking of the few kisses Lane had shared with her. "Yes, I do."

"Remember when we were kids and I told you I'd marry you someday?" He gazed at her a moment. "I tried, Callie, but it looks like you're going to end up with Hutchins. And so. . ." He shrugged. "I wish you all the best."

"Oh, Murray!" She threw her arms around his neck and gave him a quick hug. "That's the sweetest thing you've ever said to me."

"Yeah, well. . ." His face turned red, and the color crept all the way up to his red hair. He straightened up to his full height and sniffed. "Guess I'd better crack down on Bixby. Have to uphold the law, you know." He strode off toward his patrol car.

A smile lingered on Callie's lips as she watched him go. *I wish you all the best, too, Murray.*

twenty

Lane paced his jail cell, which was hard to do since it was so small. Of the four walls, three were made of bars, and a hard cot was anchored into the cement-block wall at the back. The only other cell was unoccupied. His supper, which consisted of a cold chicken leg, Styrofoam mashed potatoes, and waxy green beans, lay untouched on a tray on the cot.

The other half of the building contained a small office. Sheriff Krause sat behind his desk. Lane had never seen such a strange specimen of humanity. The sheriff's head sported a few hairs slicked down, and his sagging jowls resembled those of a bloodhound. He was a huge man who looked like he wore a life preserver around his waist. He'd probably eaten one too many doughnuts through the years. Right now he was leaning back in his chair, his hands folded over his wide girth.

He's certainly no Andy Taylor.

The front door opened, interrupting Lane's musings.

"Lane!" Callie burst into the office and ran up to his cell.

He gripped the bars. "Callie! Man, am I glad to see you."

"Now, Callie." The sheriff's chair groaned as he sat up. "If you want to visit one of the prisoners, you have to sign in." He stared at them.

"In a minute, Sheriff." Callie laid her hand over Lane's. "I've missed you."

"You wouldn't believe how much I've missed you. I'm so bored—and depressed, too." He might as well admit it.

"I'm sorry, Lane." She gripped his hand. "I have some good

news." She glanced at the sheriff. "Did Murray call you about the flower bed?"

"Yep, he told me." The sheriff got up from his chair, which creaked in protest. He stood beside Callie, making her look like a little girl, and hiked up his pants.

Lane frowned. "What does a flower bed have to do with anything?"

"Well, I visited Miss Penwell, and—"

"Did she come out of the coma?" Sheriff Krause placed his hands on his hips—or, at least, somewhere below the middle of the life preserver.

"She hasn't snapped out of it yet." Callie gazed up at Lane. "Really, I don't know if she's going to make it. But I remembered when I picked up her hand to check her pulse that there was a lot of dirt on her index finger. Murray Twichell accompanied me to the library this afternoon, and Miss Penwell had dug the initials *C. B.* in the flower bed where she was shot. Murray and I think she was trying to point out the shooter."

"*C. B.*?" Lane frowned. "Those are your initials, Callie."

"Yes, but also Chance Bixby's." She glanced at Fred. "Did Murray tell you about my visit to Chance?"

The sheriff shook his head. "What happened?"

She related the curt reception Chance had given her. "So it could be that Chance is the culprit."

"That don't prove anything, Callie." The sheriff walked back to his chair and sat down. "I'll admit that maybe—*maybe*—Lucille was trying to write something in the dirt, but you've got to have better evidence than that."

Callie folded her arms. "You don't have much evidence to hold Lane."

A siren sounded in the distance, coming closer.

The sheriff glanced out the window. "That's a highway patrol car. Must be Murray."

The siren's wail died. A few moments later, the front door opened. Chance Bixby, his wrists handcuffed behind him, walked in. He scowled at the sheriff before he spotted Lane and Callie.

Murray was right behind him. "Here's another suspect, Sheriff." He took out his keys and unlocked the cuffs. "Okay, Mr. Bixby." He placed a chair in the middle of the room. "Sit down. We need to ask you some questions."

Chance fell into the chair. He folded his arms and glared at his captors.

The sheriff stood, hiking up his pants from several places at the waistband. "Chance Bixby, where were you Thursday night, August 28?"

"Working at the library." His answer came out as a snarl.

"Did you see who shot Lucille Penwell?"

Chance opened his mouth and then closed it. He pointed at Lane. "Lucille and that man there had a real fight, Sheriff. They were yelling at each other at the top of their lungs."

Lane bowed his head. *How long will I have to relive that night?*

Callie squeezed his hand, and he looked up. *I love you,* she mouthed.

That brought a smile to his face. Someday he would marry Callie—if he didn't spend the next fifty years in jail.

The sheriff hiked up his stubborn pants. "I asked if you saw who shot Lucille."

Chance glanced around the group. "Well, I don't know. . ."

Callie left Lane's side and knelt in front of the janitor. "Chance, please, if you know anything, tell us." She motioned back to the cell. "Lane is an innocent man." She paused. "If you saw someone shoot her, we need to know."

He stared at Callie for a few seconds. "Okay, I admit it." He looked at the sheriff. "I shot Lucille."

Callie sat back on her heels with a gasp. "You did?"

The sheriff and Murray seemed as surprised as Lane felt. *That was an easy confession.*

Chance glanced around. "Yeah. Well, I'm only admitting it 'cause my conscience is bothering me terrible and 'cause of Callie." He motioned toward Lane. "I can see you like this boy, and he's suffering for something he didn't do."

"Thank you, Chance." Callie squeezed his arm, right on his anchor tattoo. "You've always been a good friend to me."

He blushed. "Aw, Callie. . ."

"You did the right thing, Bixby," the sheriff said.

Callie stepped back to Lane's side.

He grabbed her hands through the bars. "Callie, you're wonderful," he whispered. "I love you."

Wistfully, she gazed into his eyes. "I love you, too."

". . .a very serious charge," the sheriff was saying. "If Lucille dies, you will be a murderer."

Chance ran his finger around the inside of his T-shirt collar.

The sheriff nodded to Murray. "Take a few notes, Twichell."

Murray pulled out his notebook and flipped it open. "Tell us what happened, Mr. Bixby."

"If I have to." He sighed. "Lucille was in a bad mood. Probably because. . ." Chance motioned toward Lane. "When it was time to close up shop, I told her I was staying for a few hours to clean."

"Do you do that often?" The sheriff paced in front of him.

"Yeah, about once a week, and it's usually on Thursday night." He blew out a breath. "But Lucille wouldn't stand for it. She said she didn't trust me alone in the building." Chance spread his hands out. "What was I gonna do? Steal a bunch of books?"

Sheriff Krause folded his arms. "So you shot her?"

"Well, not then. We kept arguing, and she forced me out the door." Chance slapped his leg. "I got so mad—I had it up to here with that woman. I took out my pistol and pulled the trigger."

Callie leaned closer to Lane, even though the bars were in the way. He snaked his hand through the bars and patted her shoulder. He was breathing easy now.

"Do you have a permit to carry a concealed weapon, Mr. Bixby?" Murray never looked up as he continued writing.

"Sure thing! And I got it legally from the attorney general several years ago. I double as a security guard at the library, you know."

"Tell me, Bixby." Sheriff Krause stepped forward. "Did you feel any remorse for shooting Lucille Penwell?"

"Not on Thursday night. When she fell, I thought she got what she deserved."

Callie shook her head.

"But later, Friday morning, I felt bad, real bad. What had I done?" Chance's shoulders slumped. "And now I can't even sleep at night. I hope she doesn't die."

Lane actually felt sorry for the man.

The sheriff took a large ring of keys from the wall. "Okay, Bixby. Let's get in the cell." He paraded Chance past Lane's cell and opened the other one. When the door clanged shut, Chance slumped to the cot and dropped his face in his hands.

The sheriff's keys jingled as he opened Lane's cell door. "You're free to go, Mr. Hutchins."

"Thank you, sir." Feeling magnanimous, Lane shook his hand. Then he stopped to shake Murray's hand as they made their way to the door.

"Sorry about that, Hutchins—uh, Lane." Murray nodded toward Callie. "Hope everything works out for the two of you."

She smiled. "Thanks, Murray."

They walked outside. The sun was just beginning its descent in the early evening sky. Lane drew in a deep breath. "Oh, Callie, it's great to be free. Liberty is not praised enough."

She dug in her purse. "I can't believe you had to go through all that." Pulling out his car keys, she handed them to him. "It's sad that you had to suffer because of Chance's hot temper."

"I'm glad it happened."

She stared at him, her eyes wide. "You're glad you ended up in jail?"

"Sure." He threw his arm around her shoulders as they walked to the car, and she looped her arm around his waist. "I can get some good book material out of this experience. Maybe I'll write a book about the history of jails in America."

"Oh, Lane." She laughed. "That's worse than the *Gunfights* book."

He grinned as they stopped at the car. "Maybe I could interview every inmate in America who's been incarcerated on false charges." He drew his brows together. "You know, all those men who claim to be innocent?"

"There are probably a million of them." She smiled, shaking her head. "You're crazy."

"Crazy about you." He pulled her into his arms and hugged her. The sweet scent of her hair wafted under his nose. "Ah, Callie. I'm so glad God brought you into my life."

She looked up at him. "Me, too."

He kissed her lightly before opening the car door for her. In such a short time, God had changed his entire life. But there was one more thing he needed to discuss with Callie.

twenty-one

Callie sat on the passenger's seat in Lane's Mazda, thankful he was once again behind the wheel. They had eaten a good Italian dinner at Mama's Kitchen in Lusk—since Lane had not been particularly fond of jail food—and lingered at the table, discussing the entire arrest episode and talking about their childhoods. Now they were on their way back to Fort Lob. The sun had slipped below the horizon an hour ago, and the stars were out. She closed her eyes and leaned back in the seat with a contented sigh.

"You're not falling asleep, are you?"

She opened her eyes and gazed at him. The dials on the dashboard softly illuminated his face. "I'm just happy with how everything turned out. The Lord is so good."

"He certainly is." Lane grinned. "And better things are ahead, Callie. In fact, I want to discuss something with you."

Her heart leaped in her throat. She wondered how long she would have to wait before Lane proposed marriage. A few days? A few weeks? Or maybe only a few minutes. She gave a happy sigh. It didn't matter; it was in God's hands, and He had given her perfect peace about marrying Lane.

"I want to talk about the museum."

Callie's heart sank. "The museum?" Was that the *better thing* ahead? Maybe he wasn't even thinking about marriage.

He nodded. "I hope you don't mind if we make it a joint project. I'm really excited about displaying all those artifacts, all that history, to the public."

"I'd love to work with you, Lane. After all, I kind of. . .well,

I really need. . .your money."

Lane threw back his head and laughed. The sound filled the car. "No problem there. Money is no object."

Callie sighed. "Must be nice when you have plenty of money to do what you want."

"True, although I've never had anything to spend my money on before." He glanced at her. "I've just been saving it and investing some of it. That's why I can afford to pay for the renovations at the library and build you a new museum building."

"Wow, that's so amazing." She closed her eyes again.

"There's another thing I want to discuss with you."

Her eyes flew open. "Yes?"

"Tomorrow I'm going to call Mr. Porterfield."

"Oh."

"I've been talking to a book agent I met a few years ago. He didn't know I was writing as Herbert Dreyfuss back then, which is a good thing."

"Why would that be good?"

"He liked my writing and wanted to represent me when I was a nobody."

"So you trust him."

"Right you are, Callie." He grinned at her. "Along those lines, I have a book idea I'd like to bounce off you." He grew serious. "I've never had anyone I could bounce ideas off before. I usually e-mail Mr. Porterfield and tell him what I want to write for my next book, and he okays it." Lane looked at her. "If I wanted to write about the history of garbage, he would tell me to go ahead."

Callie held her nose. "That's a smelly idea."

He laughed. "See? I need someone to tell me when my ideas stink."

She couldn't help but laugh. "So what's your new book idea?"

"It would be a type of autobiography about Uncle Herb and me, with lots of photos of our family and all the things that happened in my childhood and how I started writing for him."

"Oh, I like that."

He nodded. "I'm going to title it *The Herbert Dreyfuss Story*."

She raised her eyebrows. "Not *The Lane Hutchins Story*?"

"I'll be the author." He shrugged. "My name is not even recognized in America right now. After this book gets published, I hope it is."

She laid her hand on his arm. "It will be. I have a feeling you're going to be a very famous man someday."

❧

Twenty minutes later, they drove under THE ROCKING B archway and down the long driveway.

Callie spotted Tonya's car parked beside the house. "Oh good. Mom and Tonya are back from Douglas."

Lane pulled up behind Tonya's car and parked. "Your mom's been in Douglas all these weeks?"

"Yep." Callie shrugged. "Grandma can't get around with a broken hip. Someone has to help her. My aunt is taking over for the next few weeks."

He pushed the button to roll down the front windows before turning off the ignition. "It's nice to have such a big family."

"It is." She opened the car door, and the inside light came on. "I love this summer weather. Want to sit on the porch and talk?"

"Nope." He leaned over the console between the two seats and pulled her into his arms. "I don't want to sit there because we might get interrupted like we did before, and I think we've talked enough this evening." As he said the words, he drew closer until his lips touched hers.

That kiss made Callie's toes curl in her shoes.

This was where she belonged, right here in Lane's arms. She hoped he didn't have a commitment phobia like her brother.

When they parted, he gazed at her in the twilight. "You've helped me so much, Callie. I can't begin to repay you."

She raised her eyebrows. "But you are repaying me. Remember? The library and the museum?"

"That's kid stuff. Actually, I can't imagine my life without you now."

Callie felt like her heart would burst. "Oh, neither can I, Lane." A warm breeze blew through the open door, lifting her hair across her face.

Lane brushed it back and drew in a deep breath. "I can't get on my knees in the car, and I don't have a ring—but will you marry me, Callie?"

Yes! "Oh, Lane." Unexpected tears filled her eyes. "I wanted to marry you the first day I met you at the library."

He lifted his brows. "Really?"

"I know now that I couldn't marry just anybody who walked in off the street, but God planted that desire for you in my heart." She gazed into his eyes. "Yes, Lane, I want to marry you."

He leaned over and kissed her again then lifted his head. "You know, this would be a lot easier if we weren't sitting in the car."

She laughed and grabbed his hand. "Come in the house. Mom and Dad think you're still in jail." She gave a happy sigh. "We have so much to tell them."

epilogue

"Oh, Callie!" Agatha Collingsworth stood by the big plate glass windows of The Beauty Spot and looked out on Elk Road. "It's snowing, sugar. Ya'll are gonna have a white wedding."

"It's snowing?" Callie swiveled in the beautician's chair to look outside. "Wow! It's really coming down. And I can *see* those snowflakes."

Tonya pulled a curl from the top of her sister's head. "Callie, turn back and face the mirror."

"Sorry." Callie gazed back at her reflection. Tonya stood behind her, piling her hair on top of her head and pinning it, one curl at a time. "I still can't believe how well I can see without my glasses."

Watching Tonya work, Aggie plopped down in the other beautician's chair. "That was so nice of Lane to give ya that laser eye surgery as a wedding present."

"Isn't the Lord good?" Callie gave a wistful sigh. "I always wanted to have laser surgery but never thought it would be a reality." She frowned. "Now I feel bad. All I gave him for a wedding gift was a tie clasp."

Aggie cackled out a laugh. "Hon, he could buy himself a hundred tie clasps, but this one was from you. He'll treasure it always."

"It's the thought that counts." Tonya pinned another curl.

"I guess so."

Aggie stood, frowning. "Now, sugar, look at your lips. They need some color." She opened a drawer beneath the mirror. "Here, try this one. Radiant Sunset."

"But I haven't even put on my makeup yet."

"Won't hurt to test it." Aggie handed her the lipstick tube.

Callie dutifully opened the tube and painted her lips. Aggie had already given her a free manicure and had applied two coats of Dusty Rose polish to her nails. *Now she's going to work on my face.*

Callie looked in the mirror. Her lips were orange. "I don't think this is my color."

Tonya's hands stilled as she glanced at Callie's reflection. "It's too orange, Aggie. She needs something lighter and more pink."

"Looks good to me," Aggie muttered. She rummaged in the drawer.

"A lot lighter." Callie sighed under her breath. Aggie was being a little too helpful.

The bell over the door jangled, and all three women turned. A blast of cold air accompanied Cheyenne as she entered the small waiting area.

"Hi, girls!" She removed her coat and shook off the snow. "We were praying for snow for your wedding day, and look how God answered prayer."

Callie smiled. Her wedding day. She liked the sound of those words.

Cheyenne sat down in the other chair. "Wow, Callie, you are going to be one beautiful bride."

"Except for her orange lips." Tonya laughed.

"Here, hon." Aggie handed Callie a tissue. "Blot that one off and try this. It's called Blushing Rose."

Aggie turned back to the drawer, and Callie rolled her eyes.

Cheyenne grinned. "Are you nervous, girlfriend?"

"Not too much. I still have so much to do before tonight. Mom and I are picking up the cake at three—Alice is making it—and the flowers are supposed to arrive at the church at five."

"I hope this snow doesn't turn into a blizzard." Tonya pulled on Callie's hair. "That would be terrible if the florist couldn't get over to the church from Douglas."

No flowers! "That would be terrible." Callie sent up a silent prayer for the florist deliveryman.

"It'll be something to tell your grandchildren someday." Cheyenne crossed her legs, and her jeans were wet on the bottom edges. "Fifty years ago on December 5, we had a huge blizzard! Why, the snow just swirled and whirled around the florist's delivery van. We never thought he'd make it."

Callie groaned. "Save the theatrics, Cheyenne."

Tonya laughed. "The weather can change fast in Wyoming. Last night it was so clear, even though it was cold."

"Yeah, cold and clear." Aggie handed Callie another lipstick tube. "Try this, sugar. Pink Carnation."

Thinking back to the clear skies last night, Callie couldn't help but smile as she applied the lipstick. When Lane had kissed her good night, he said, "This is the last night I'm going to leave you." Tonight they planned to spend their wedding night in a fancy hotel in Douglas. In a few days, they would drive to Yellowstone National Park for their honeymoon. Lane had rented a cozy cabin for them, and Callie couldn't wait.

Aggie peered at her. "That's your color, sugar." She grinned. "You'll be a beautiful bride, hon, just like Cheyenne said."

Tonya sighed. "I wish I was getting married. You're so lucky, Callie."

"Luck had nothing to do with it." Callie met her sister's eyes in the mirror. "God brought us together."

"Now Tonya. . ." Aggie cackled. "Don't you worry none. God will bring your man along soon enough."

Cheyenne folded her arms. "At least you have guys who ask you out, Tonya. Look at me." She stood. "Almost six feet tall and pudgy all over. Who would want to date an Amazon?"

"Don't say that, Chey." Callie bit her lip, wishing she could wipe the lipstick off. "We're still praying about you and Derek."

Cheyenne took her seat. "I've given up on Derek."

"What?" In unison, Callie and Tonya stared at her.

"It's impossible. He's never going to marry me."

"Yes, he is." Callie glanced back at her reflection. "If God could give me Lane, He can give you Derek. You need to have faith." She smiled. "Besides, I've always wanted you to be my sister-in-law."

"All finished." Tonya twirled Callie's chair around so she faced Cheyenne and Aggie. "What do you think?"

"Cool 'do." Cheyenne smiled. "You did a great job, Tonya. I wish I could fix hair like that."

Aggie frowned, tapping a lipstick tube against her double chin. "That color is still not right." She thrust the tube under Callie's nose. "Try this one. Light Fuchsia."

❧

At exactly seven o'clock that evening, Lane followed Pastor Reilly from a side room to the front of the church auditorium. Derek and his brother, Ryan, plus two cousins whom Lane had just met yesterday, followed behind him.

The men stood at the front of the church, waiting. The strains of the organ played in the background, but Lane barely heard the music. The church was filled with hundreds of lit candles—the only light in the room—and an abundance of red and white roses surrounded the altar. A few stragglers were seated in the back row of the packed auditorium.

Lane looked over the congregation. There was Vern Snyder and his wife. The man was actually civil now, but Lane was still surprised he had come. It was probably one of those situations where the Snyders were friends of the Brandt family and had been for years. Weddings and funerals seemed to draw people together, especially in small towns.

Near the front, Lane spotted Lucille Penwell. She had awoken from her comatose state five days after the shooting and made a rapid recovery. While she was still in the hospital, Callie talked to her several times about her eternal destiny, and Miss Penwell accepted Christ as her Savior. God had totally changed that woman. Now she actually liked Lane.

Bruce MacKinnon sat a few rows behind Miss Penwell, and Lane couldn't stop the rush of gratitude that flowed through him. In the last three months, Bruce had convinced the town council to give Lane and Callie ten acres of property on the outskirts of Fort Lob for the museum. They also voted—unanimously—to donate everything from the library's third floor. Plans were on the drawing board for the building. Lane planned to supervise the construction, and he had already purchased a house in town on Little Deer Road for himself and his bride. They had spent the past three weeks buying furniture, and Callie had a blast decorating the house.

As far as telling the world that he was Herbert Dreyfuss, Lane finally confessed it in his newspaper column a month ago. He had given his e-mail address and had been flooded with thousands of letters supporting him. God had worked everything out for good.

Lane pulled his wandering thoughts back to his wedding and glanced down at the front row. Yvette Brandt, his future mother-in-law, sat by an empty space reserved for Jake. Callie's grandmother, healed from her broken hip, sat beside Yvette. A host of relatives filled the first seven pews, and Lane was still trying to keep everyone straight.

Yvette caught his eye and gave a little wave. Lane smiled back. He finally belonged to a family.

The organ music changed, and Melissa, Callie's oldest sister, started down the aisle. The audience turned in their pews, craning their necks to watch her. She wore a deep red velvet dress with a white fur collar and carried a small bouquet of red and white roses.

Lane watched Melissa ascend the platform, then he turned to wait for Molly, her twin. He thought the twins looked just like their dad, Jake. Callie and Tonya looked more like their mom, and of course, Callie was the most beautiful of the sisters.

She's the most beautiful woman in this church—no, in the world.

Cheyenne walked down the aisle next, and she winked at Lane as she ascended the steps. He grinned, knowing that Cheyenne had wanted him to marry Callie from the beginning.

Tonya, the maid of honor, followed Cheyenne down the aisle. Then the music changed to "Here Comes the Bride." Lane didn't recognize any of the other music, but he knew that song. He could see Callie and her dad standing at the entrance of the auditorium. She looked beautiful in her white bridal gown, which Lane had helped her pick out. Even now he remembered how bored he was, waiting for Callie to pop out of the dressing room in yet another wedding gown. As far as he was concerned, she could have worn a gunnysack and she would be beautiful. But now he gazed at her, drinking in her beauty in yards of white satin with a shiny tiara nestled in her hair.

Callie's eyes met his—those beautiful eyes, unshackled from her glasses. In a few minutes, she and her dad were at the front, and Jake was giving his daughter away—to him.

Lane drew a deep breath, hardly able to believe this was happening. He was getting married!

❧

Callie stood beside Lane, pledging her life to him. Her flowers quivered a little, and she hoped she wouldn't cry. She had dreamed of this day for years but didn't think it would ever happen. She always figured she would end up like Miss Penwell, still single in her seventies, working in the library.

But God had other plans.

As Callie gazed into Lane's eyes, she knew God's purpose for her life was right here by his side. She repeated the wedding vows, meaning every word, amazed how God had orchestrated everything to bring them together. They had met at the library, and it seemed all that happened in the past four months revolved around that old mansion and their mutual love of books.

Now Lane would be a celebrated author in his own right, and she would be able, finally, to realize her dream of having a bookstore, plus a museum for the town of Fort Lob.

She wiped a tear from her eye as Pastor Reilly pronounced them man and wife. Lane pulled her into his arms and kissed her, and that kiss held the promise of a lifetime.

The pastor cleared his throat. "I now introduce to you Mr. and Mrs. Lane Hutchins."

The refrain of "The Wedding March" burst from the organ, and applause erupted from the audience as Callie and Lane walked down the aisle.

Alone in the lobby, Callie threw her arms around his neck. "I can't believe we're married!"

"This is just the beginning, Callie." His arms tightened around her. "I expect to cherish you my whole life."

She breathed a happy sigh. "God is so good."

"Yes, He is." Lane leaned back to look her in the eye. "Far better than I deserve. But it's like that verse in Philippians says—'It is God which worketh in you both to will and to do of his good pleasure.'"

As Callie laid her head against his shoulder, she glanced out the glass door of the church. Snow drifted down outside against the streetlight, and she felt God's peace fill her.

Lord, You gave me a love of books. Thank You for also giving me the love of my life.

A Letter To Our Readers

Dear Reader:
In order that we might better contribute to your reading enjoyment, we would appreciate your taking a few minutes to respond to the following questions. We welcome your comments and read each form and letter we receive. When completed, please return to the following:

Fiction Editor
Heartsong Presents
PO Box 719
Uhrichsville, Ohio 44683

1. Did you enjoy reading *For the Love of Books* by Donna Reimel Robinson?
   - ❑ Very much! I would like to see more books by this author!
   - ❑ Moderately. I would have enjoyed it more if

   ____

   ____

   ____

2. Are you a member of **Heartsong Presents**? ❑ Yes ❑ No
   If no, where did you purchase this book? ________________

   ____

3. How would you rate, on a scale from 1 (poor) to 5 (superior), the cover design? ______________________________

4. On a scale from 1 (poor) to 10 (superior), please rate the following elements.

____ Heroine	____ Plot
____ Hero	____ Inspirational theme
____ Setting	____ Secondary characters

5. These characters were special because? ______________

____

____

6. How has this book inspired your life? ______________

____

____

7. What settings would you like to see covered in future **Heartsong Presents** books? ______________

____

____

8. What are some inspirational themes you would like to see treated in future books? ______________

____

____

9. Would you be interested in reading other **Heartsong Presents** titles? ❑ Yes ❑ No

10. Please check your age range:

❑ Under 18	❑ 18-24
❑ 25-34	❑ 35-45
❑ 46-55	❑ Over 55

Name ____

Occupation ______________________________________

Address ____

City, State, Zip __________________________________